Short Trip to the Grave . . .

Another shot rang out, the bullet clipping the top of the headstone and whining off into the distance in the direction of the church behind them.

"Ah, there you are," Longarm mumbled, glaring toward the puff of white gunsmoke that marked the position of the shooter.

He again reached down to give Georgia a reassuring touch on her back, then gathered himself and sprinted for the next tombstone.

The gunman fired a third shot. This time the bullet came close enough for Longarm to hear the sizzle of its passage through the air. He lifted the derringer on its tether and squeezed off a shot toward the puff of gunsmoke forty yards or so ahead. His object was not to kill—although that would certainly be a welcome fluke—but to let the son of a bitch know that Longarm intended to attack, not just hide behind one grave while waiting to be put into one of his own . . .

DON'T MISS THESE
ALL-ACTION WESTERN SERIES
FROM THE BERKLEY PUBLISHING GROUP

THE GUNSMITH by J. R. Roberts
Clint Adams was a legend among lawmen, outlaws, and ladies. They called him . . . the Gunsmith.

LONGARM by Tabor Evans
The popular long-running series about Deputy U.S. Marshal Custis Long—his life, his loves, his fight for justice.

SLOCUM by Jake Logan
Today's longest-running action Western. John Slocum rides a deadly trail of hot blood and cold steel.

BUSHWHACKERS by B. J. Lanagan
An action-packed series by the creators of Longarm! The rousing adventures of the most brutal gang of cutthroats ever assembled—Quantrill's Raiders.

DIAMONDBACK by Guy Brewer
Dex Yancey is Diamondback, a Southern gentleman turned con man when his brother cheats him out of the family fortune. Ladies love him. Gamblers hate him. But nobody pulls one over on Dex . . .

WILDGUN by Jack Hanson
The blazing adventures of mountain man Will Barlow—from the creators of Longarm!

TEXAS TRACKER by Tom Calhoun
J.T. Law: the most relentless—and dangerous—manhunter in all Texas. Where sheriffs and posses fail, he's the best man to bring in the most vicious outlaws—for a price.

→ TABOR EVANS ←

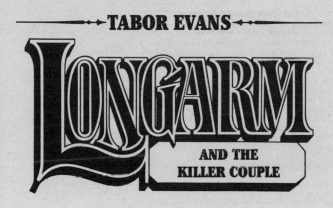

LONGARM

AND THE
KILLER COUPLE

JOVE BOOKS, NEW YORK

THE BERKLEY PUBLISHING GROUP
Published by the Penguin Group
Penguin Group (USA) Inc.
375 Hudson Street, New York, New York 10014, USA
Penguin Group (Canada), 90 Eglinton Avenue East, Suite 700, Toronto, Ontario M4P 2Y3, Canada
(a division of Pearson Penguin Canada Inc.)
Penguin Books Ltd., 80 Strand, London WC2R 0RL, England
Penguin Group Ireland, 25 St. Stephen's Green, Dublin 2, Ireland (a division of Penguin Books Ltd.)
Penguin Group (Australia), 250 Camberwell Road, Camberwell, Victoria 3124, Australia
(a division of Pearson Australia Group Pty. Ltd.)
Penguin Books India Pvt. Ltd., 11 Community Centre, Panchsheel Park, New Delhi—110 017, India
Penguin Group (NZ), 67 Apollo Drive, Rosedale, North Shore 0632, New Zealand
(a division of Pearson New Zealand Ltd.)
Penguin Books (South Africa) (Pty.) Ltd., 24 Sturdee Avenue, Rosebank, Johannesburg 2196,
South Africa

Penguin Books Ltd., Registered Offices: 80 Strand, London WC2R 0RL, England

This is a work of fiction. Names, characters, places, and incidents either are the product of the author's imagination or are used fictitiously, and any resemblance to actual persons, living or dead, business establishments, events, or locales is entirely coincidental.

LONGARM AND THE KILLER COUPLE

A Jove Book / published by arrangement with the author

PRINTING HISTORY
Jove edition / April 2011

Copyright © 2011 by Penguin Group (USA) Inc.
Cover illustration by Miro Sinovcic.

ISBN: 978-0-515-14927-2

JOVE®
Jove Books are published by The Berkley Publishing Group,
a division of Penguin Group (USA) Inc.,
375 Hudson Street, New York, New York 10014.
JOVE® is a registered trademark of Penguin Group (USA) Inc.
The "J" design is a trademark of Penguin Group (USA) Inc.

PRINTED IN THE UNITED STATES OF AMERICA

10   9   8   7   6   5   4   3   2   1

Chapter 1

Custis Long woke slowly, a vile taste in his mouth. Funny, he thought, how whiskey that tastes so good in the evening going down tastes so terrible in the morning coming back up. Not that he was considering quitting, but still . . .

He rolled over, smacking his lips and yawning. He felt good. Everything considered, that is. At least his headache was only a very small one and not the volcanic head-splitter that came from bad whiskey. The logical conclusion was that he had been drinking good stuff last night. Not that he could exactly remember, but still . . .

He yawned again and squeezed the warm pillow that his hand had come to rest on.

Warm pillow. With a bulge on top. A bulge that seemed to be growing larger.

He felt of the rubbery protrusion. Examined it with his fingertips. It was warm. It was . . . Damned if it did not feel exactly like a nipple. A rather large nipple at that.

Long's eyes snapped open to be confronted with a tit. A really, really *big* tit. A tit, in fact, of almost colossal size.

And another just like it that he had been lying on, thinking it was a pillow.

He shifted his gaze northward just a little distance and discovered that he was in bed with a blond female. A truly *large* blond female. In fact a grossly *fat* blond female.

Who she was and how he'd wound up in her bed—at least he assumed it was her bed as it for damn sure was not his—was a mystery to him, a mystery that he did not think he wanted explained.

If he could just slip away without waking her . . .

"Custis. Sweetheart."

All right, so he was not going to get away without waking this fat blond female. But perhaps he could . . .

"Dearie!"

He felt a light touch as she cupped his balls and gently kneaded his cock into a morning erection, that being a chore that was not particularly difficult to accomplish. Pretty much any friendly touch in that neighborhood was likely to give the same result, that being a hard-on that a cat couldn't scratch.

"Sweet thing." She had a hoarse, slightly raspy voice.

She sat upright, taking his pillow-tit with her so that his head dropped down onto a firm mattress hard enough to make him wince. The minor headache turned into a major one.

The woman—who the hell was she anyway and what might her name be?—bent over, engulfing his midsection with a mound of warm fat and tit. It felt . . . not bad actually.

Her tits, each one as big as a bucket, surrounded his dick. She pressed them together and began rubbing the two back and forth with his cock trapped between them.

Long supposed he should object but . . . damn, it felt good.

The blond woman let go of her own tits and pulled back

a little, one hand sliding down to cup his balls while one fingertip teased his tight puckered asshole.

She bent lower, her jowls and the wattles on her neck hanging loose when she did so.

He closed his eyes to blot out the sight.

At the same time he felt a delightful warmth envelop his dick as the ugly woman took his cock into her mouth.

He supposed he should object, but still . . .

She suckled slowly, stroking his shaft and tickling his balls until he felt the sweet sap begin to rise down deep, more and more insistently, until he could contain it no longer and it exploded up the length of his shaft and out, into the fat woman's mouth.

She sucked even harder then, drawing out the full flow of his fluid and swallowing it down, staying with him even after the last drops were gone and the sensations were so intense as to be almost painful.

"Enough," he said. "Enough."

The woman laughed, joy evident in the tone of it. She sat up and caressed his thigh. "Now me," she said.

"What?"

"It's your turn, dearie. Now you lick my pussy." She lay back and spread wide the heavy hams that served as her legs, exposing a hank of wet, curly hair and a cunt that looked like Sherman's army could bivouac inside it . . . and very well might have.

The man who was known as Longarm, the man who was United States marshal Billy Vail's top deputy, this man who had survived countless gunfights and overcome innumerable criminals, felt his stomach churn with dread, and cold sweat break out on his cheeks and forehead.

That cunt looked just plain *nasty*!

"Come to Katie, sweet darlin'." She reached for the back of his head and pulled him toward her crotch.

Chapter 2

"Good morning, Longarm. Say, you don't look so good. Are you all right?"

"Fine, Henry. Top o' the world," he lied to Billy Vail's frail-looking office clerk. The truth was that Longarm felt like he had been run over by a wagon. Hell, several wagons. In fact he wished he *had* been run over by a wagon instead of winding up—somehow—with that creature from Kelly's Bar and Grill, where she presided over the bar part.

"If I may say so, Longarm, you look like shit."

"Thank you, Henry. 'S kind of you to say that."

"Don't take offense now."

"Nope. None taken." Longarm belched, flavors from the previous night unpleasant in his mouth now. "I hope like hell the boss don't have anything for me today. I feel like crawling into a hole an' pulling the dirt in over me."

"Sorry, Custis. You have work to do."

Longarm sighed. "All right then. Tell him I'm here."

"You don't have to see him unless you need to for some other reason," Henry said. "It's a simple job so he told me to take care of it."

Longarm nodded. He was familiar with the matter, robbery of the mail, but had not been personally involved. Billy
would be helping lay out the prosecution now. "So what is
it I have to do?"

"Easy pickings this time, Longarm. Prisoner transport is
all. The U.S. attorney has decided to pass Charlie Cade along
to Tillet County for prosecution on state charges there. After all, all we have on him is the theft of seventy-five cents'
worth of postage stamps. They want to prosecute him for
assault and battery."

Henry opened a desk drawer and brought out a folder,
then opened it and selected a slim sheaf of papers that he
extended to Longarm. "Here's your travel voucher and the
writ to get him out of lockup. You're to take Charlie over to
Sheriff . . . Let me see, I have it written down right, um, oh
yes, right here . . . Sheriff Jim Todd. Have Todd sign this,"
Henry selected another paper from the folder and gave it to
Longarm, "then come back. Like I said. Easy."

"Easy enough," Longarm said. He meant it and was grate-
ful for it. If he had to work with a hangover, this was the
best he might have hoped for. But how he had managed to
end up in fat Katie's bed . . . It was probably just as well
that he did not know.

"You should be back in just a few days," Henry said. "I'll
try to have something more interesting for you by then." The
slender clerk smiled and used a fingertip to push his specta-
cles higher on his nose, a gesture that had become a habit
with him whether he needed to reposition them or not.

Longarm yawned and straightened his shoulders. He
was a tall man, several inches over six feet in height. He
had broad shoulders, a narrow waist, thick, brown hair, and
a large mustache to match. His features were more rugged
than handsome, but there was something in him, a wildness
perhaps, that caused him to appeal to women.

He wore a flat-crowned brown Stetson, brown tweed coat, calfskin vest, and brown corduroy trousers with black stove-pipe boots. He had a double-action Colt .45 in a cross-draw holster set just to the left of his belt buckle, and a hideout derringer in his vest pocket, at the end of a watch chain.

And at the moment he felt so shaky that he was not sure he could hit a bull in the ass if he was sitting on top of the critter.

"Henry, I've just about had it. Too much liquor an' too many women. I need a few days t' unwind a little. I know I got some time coming to me, so while I'm up there in Tillet County I'm gonna take a few days off. Maybe go fishing or something. They got some fine mountain streams up that way. I may just park myself alongside o' one and get me some rest."

"All right, Longarm. I won't bother the boss with anything official. Just take a couple days. If anything comes up, I'll handle it until you get back."

Longarm smiled. "You're a pal, Henry." He laughed then, already feeling better. "And I don't care what all them other deputies say behind your back, you're all right with me."

"Get out of here, you idiot. And don't forget to bring back that signed transfer form for my records."

Chapter 3

Longarm gave the nod to a hansom driver waiting in front of the Mint on Colfax Avenue. He went home to his boardinghouse to collect his carpetbag, but left his saddle and Winchester there. Charles Cade was not a violent criminal, and besides Longarm did not want to be burdened with excess baggage to drag along. Watching over a prisoner, even an agreeable one, would occupy his attention quite enough without having to think about those objects too.

"All right now," he told the driver when he emerged from the boarding house, "let's go on to the Whitworth Express depot."

Longarm climbed into the cab and barely had time to get seated before the driver snapped his whip over the ears of the short-coupled brown cob and they rocked into motion, traveling back across Cherry Creek and north to the stage company's Denver location.

Longarm paid the driver—and made a mental note to put that on his expense sheet—and went inside to a ticket window where a bored clerk in sleeve garters and green celluloid eyeshade was reading a newspaper.

"Yes, sir?"

Longarm identified himself and said, "When's your next coach going to Buffington?"

"That would be this afternoon at four-fifteen. It arrives in Buffington at three in the afternoon, day after tomorrow."

Longarm grunted. It was a lousy schedule, but it was what was available. "Is it full?"

"No, sir. I only have two passengers so far."

"Now you have two more," Longarm told the man. "Government business."

"Yes, sir. No charge but you will need tickets."

"I'll take those now. And I'd like to leave my bag here."

"I'll have it put aboard for you, sir."

"Fine, thanks." Longarm handed over his carpetbag and said, "I'll go get my prisoner now and be back in time to catch that coach."

The clerk stamped a pair of tickets and gave them to Longarm. "We'll board about four, sir."

"We'll be here." Longarm touched the brim of his Stetson and went back outside. The same hansom that had brought him to the depot was still outside waiting for another fare, so Longarm climbed into that one again for the drive to the jail, where he had no need to show his credentials.

"What brings you here today, Longarm? Putting one in or taking one out?" the head jailer asked when Longarm walked in.

"Taking one off your hands this time, Bertram. Cade, Charles. In for petty theft."

"Sign here," the jailer said, pushing a logbook across the counter. "You know the drill."

"Indeed I do, Bertram, indeed I do." Longarm signed where he had to, initialed a few other places, and signed two more forms while jail personnel went into the depths of the building and returned with the prisoner.

Charlie Cade proved to be a man of middling height with unkempt black hair, a pencil mustache that was badly in need of trimming, and side whiskers that extended down along his jawline. He was wearing a suit, shoes instead of boots, and an old-fashioned beaver top hat.

"Now what?" he asked after Longarm introduced himself.

Longarm explained. Cade merely shrugged at the news. "I suppose it doesn't matter whose jail I have to sit in," he said, "yours, theirs, or somebody else's."

"Look at the bright side," Longarm said. "Maybe you'll be acquitted."

"No chance," Cade said, shaking his head. "Things have turned bad for me. I can feel it."

"You'll feel better about things with a hot meal under your belt. Better yet with a haircut and shave. We have time for that if you like. D'you have any money?"

"Not a sou," Cade told him.

"Well I do. I'm willing to front you the price of a visit to the barber while we're waiting for that stagecoach to roll."

"That's nice of you, Deputy."

"You're welcome. But you will be traveling in manacles while we're together. Nothing personal, mind. No offense intended."

"None taken," Cade said.

Longarm put handcuffs on him and said, "Let's go then. What would you prefer first, the barber or a restaurant?"

Chapter 4

Longarm and his much more civilized-appearing prisoner were waiting on the sidewalk when the jehu pulled the coach around from the stables. The rig looked like a poor man's imitation of the famous Concord coaches, similar in shape but smaller and not so handsomely made as a genuine Concord. It was drawn by a four-up of stout cobs. The driver was a young fellow barely old enough to shave, but he handled his team like he knew what he was doing and that was all that mattered.

"Everybody aboard for points south and west," he called from his perch on the elevated driving box.

A pair of weary-looking men wearing city clothing stepped forward. Longarm and Cade dropped in behind them as they climbed awkwardly into the coach.

There was no middle seat in this small version of the standard stagecoach, Longarm found, only padded benches, one facing forward and another facing toward the rear. Each bench was wide enough to seat three passengers.

The drummers—if that was what they were—chose separate benches. Longarm motioned Cade to a forward-facing seat. He climbed in and settled onto the rear-facing bench. At the last moment a young woman wearing a linen duster over her dress came dashing out of the office and joined the travelers. Longarm offered his hand to help her in, and she gave him a smile, then squeezed onto the seat at his side.

From what little he could see through her veil the woman was not very pretty, but she certainly smelled nice. Her perfume was strong enough to make a man's eyes water. How she managed to put up with the stink of it, trapped inside that veil, he could not understand.

But then there was a hell of a lot about women that he could not claim to really understand.

The ticket clerk came out to take a cursory glance at the tickets before he pulled the steps up and slid them into place underneath the body of the coach. He pushed the door closed, made sure it was securely latched, and called up to the driver, "Ready below, Hank."

"Then hold on to your teeth, folks," the driver returned. He snapped his whip and the four cobs leaned into their harness. The coach lurched ahead on its leather springs, swaying back and forth sideways for seemingly as much distance as the coach rolled forward. "Next stop Castle Rock."

Longarm settled into a sort of doze, resting but ready to jump if Charlie Cade tried to wander off on his own.

This would be a long trip, he thought, and a boring one.

He was wrong, at least about the boring part.

Chapter 5

Longarm woke up with a foul taste in his mouth and a crick in his neck from having it at an awkward angle while he slept. It was . . . He had no idea what time it might be. Sometime in the middle of the night. He dipped a hand into his coat pocket, trying as best he was able to avoid disturbing the woman beside him, and brought out a sulfur-tipped lucifer.

He dragged his Ingersoll out of the vest pocket opposite the one that held his derringer, snapped the match aflame with a fingernail, and checked the face of the faithful watch. They were minutes short of midnight, which meant they were somewhere in the San Juan Mountains. Longarm quickly extinguished the match and tossed it out the coach window. He did not want to disturb any of the other passengers, all of whom seemed to be sleeping.

He looked outside but could see nothing, not even stars. Apparently there was a heavy overcast making the night about as dark as dark could get. He hoped the driver—or more likely the horses pulling the rig—could see where the hell they were going because there were some damned well spectacular roads down this way. One misstep by one horse could send the whole outfit tumbling down several hundred feet or more, and that could thoroughly screw up a fellow's day.

Up above he could hear the driver cussing and encouraging the team. But not, Longarm noticed, using his whip, suggesting that the road here was a real son of a bitch.

They rolled on for perhaps another ten minutes, then began to slow as the grade steepened and the horses tired. At the top of whatever pass this was, the jehu pulled the rig to a halt.

"Get down an' chain the off rear, Jimmy," Longarm heard the man—their fourth driver since leaving Denver—say to the shotgun messenger.

"In a jiffy," the unseen Jimmy responded.

"Take your time. I want to give these horses a breather before we start down."

The coach rocked to the side a little as Jimmy climbed down to the ground. A moment later Longarm heard him unlatch the luggage boot, followed by the rattle of chain.

And a moment after that a new voice cut through the night.

"Stand and deliver!" That voice was harsh, cold, and commanding.

"Yes, sir," the jehu said. And just as well too. His horses were not going to outrun anyone on these roads. Including someone on foot, more than likely. He would risk the coach and everyone in it if he tried to run the team downhill in the dark and with that wheel not yet locked. Besides which, his shotgun guard was standing at the back of the coach, and there was no chance he would have bothered to take his shotgun with him when he climbed down to attend to that wheel. No, the coach and its driver were at the mercy of the highwayman giving the orders out there.

"No, don't do that, driver. Do not throw down that bag,"

the voice instructed. "Put it back where it was," and seconds later, "Good. Now just stay as you are and everything will be fine. A few minutes and you can get back on your run like nothing ever happened."

"Yes, sir. You, uh, you don't want the mailbag?" Disbelief was plain in the driver's voice.

"Absolutely not. Now, you inside," the voice called. "Charles Cade. Are you awake?"

Probably everyone in the coach would be awake by now, Longarm suspected, including the woman who still sat close beside him and the three rough-looking mining men who had replaced the two drummers back in Pueblo. The miners, if that was what they were, spoke a language Longarm did not recognize. Polish, perhaps, or some similar tongue. They seemed to have very little English.

"I'm awake," Cade returned.

"Come on out, Charlie. We've come to free you."

"Lou? Is that you, Lou?"

"No names, Charlie. There's a U.S. marshal in there with you, and we don't want them after us for assault on one of their kind."

"I'm coming out," Cade quickly shouted.

Longarm already had his hand resting lightly on the butt of his .45. "No you aren't, Charlie," he said softly. "Stay right where you are."

Longarm felt a sudden pressure low on his right side. Just forward of where his kidneys would be.

"Yes, he is," a sweetly feminine voice corrected. "What you feel is the muzzle of a rather large-caliber pistol. I'll not hesitate to pull the trigger if I must, but I would prefer not to. Now, sir, please hand me your pistol." Longarm did as she asked. He hated it. But he did it.

She raised her voice a little and said, "Go ahead, Charlie. I'll follow when you are clear."

Cade untangled himself from the feet of the Poles and climbed over Longarm's knees, pushed the door open and paused a moment to say, "You've treated me square, Deputy. Thanks." Then he was gone into the night, the coach again swaying a little with the change of weight distribution.

"Mister, you can get back onto the box," the voice said, presumably to the guard. "But you'd best leave your shotgun be. In fact, you, driver."

"Yes, sir?"

"Toss that gun down. We don't want any heroes here. Don't want anyone hurt."

"All right. Coming down now."

The pressure in Longarm's ribs increased a little as the woman pressed more insistently. "Just stay right where you are and everything will be fine," the lady said. She leaned forward, stood up as well as one could inside the confines of the stagecoach and stepped over Longarm's legs.

A shadowy figure reached up to steady the woman's arm as she climbed down to the ground.

The coach door was closed, and the deep, masculine voice said, "You can get on with your run, driver. Sorry to have detained you."

The jehu urged his team forward even though that right rear wheel had not yet been chained.

"Easy, boys, easy," he cooed.

Longarm's fingertips caressed the bulge in his vest that was his .41-caliber derringer.

Two shots, he concluded, were not enough to take on whatever gang it was that had rescued Charles Cade from his custody. He had little choice but to stay with the coach as far as the next town.

But after that . . .

Chapter 6

The next town down the line was a tiny mining community made up of a dozen or so crudely built log structures scattered along the banks of a sparkling little stream. The stream held scores of men bending over gravel pans or swishing water and mud out of them in the dip-and-circle movement required of the placer miner.

In addition to the log buildings, the surrounding trees—what of them that had not yet been cut down for building materials or firewood—held an assortment of tents, lean-tos, and tarpaulins to provide shelter to the ever hopeful miners.

Standing knee-deep in an icy mountain creek, back breaking and arms weary . . . not Custis Long's idea of a good time or even a good job. But these men had hopes and dreams and ambitions. Longarm admired them for that, even though he had no desire to join them in their quest for "easy" riches.

It had been a slow trip down from the summit thanks to all the wheels being free. They had to ease their way down practically step by step to keep the coach from running up onto the wheelers' hocks. Now the stagecoach was trying to make up time. They rolled right on through this rough-and-ready camp, prompting Longarm to call up to the driver, "Whoa up here. Aren't we going to stop?"

"No need," the driver returned.

"Stop, please. I need to get off."

Their speed almost immediately slackened, and then came to a halt as the driver hauled back on his lines. Longarm opened the coach door and dropped to the ground without waiting for the steps to be placed.

"Are you sure you know what you're doing, mister? There's no law to report the holdup to. Closest law that I know about is over to Buffington and that's hours away yet." The man reached into a coat pocket and brought out a plug of tobacco. He bit off a chunk and relinquished his plug to the shotgun messenger, who helped himself to a chew as well.

"Fact is, friend, I *am* the law," Longarm told him, "and I figure to go back there and see what I can see. Meantime, you go ahead and report this to Sheriff Jim Todd. Ask him to send out a posse to back me up." He grinned. "If I ain't got it all worked out yet. Now, toss me down that carpetbag yonder. That's it, hard against the nigh rail. Yes, that's it. Thank you."

Longarm extracted a cheroot from his inside pocket, bit the twist off, and thumbed a match aflame. He dipped his head to bring the cut end of the slim cigar down to the flame and took a pull on the cheroot before he touched a finger to the brim of his Stetson in salute to the driver and turned away from the stagecoach, alone and afoot somewhere in the mountains of southwest Colorado.

The largest of the log structures had a split aspen plank spiked above the door with the single word "Supplies" burned into the pale wood. Longarm headed for it. He had to duck his head to enter without braining himself. Or at least knocking his hat off his head.

"Hello? Anybody here?" The place appeared to be empty. Not that there was much that anyone might want to steal. The supplies on offer were meager. A few kegs and barrels, stacks of flannel shirts and denim overalls, sacks of jerky and root vegetables like turnips and rutabagas, onions and potatoes, even some dry husks of corn. Longarm's nose wrinkled with distaste when he saw the turnips and the rutabagas. He could not much abide either of those. "Hello?" he called again.

"Right behind you," a gruff voice said.

Longarm spun around, startled. A man stood there, dripping water from his lower legs onto the dirt—but rapidly turning to mud—floor. He was silhouetted against the daylight beyond the doorway, so all Longarm could see was a rather bulky outline.

"What can I do you for, mister?" He sounded friendly enough.

"Are you the, uh, proprietor here?"

"That I am." The fellow extended his hand and came forward. Once he was fully inside, Longarm could see him better. He turned out to be a plump, graying fellow with a full spade beard and a wool cap pulled down to his ears.

Longarm shook hands with the gent and introduced himself.

"I'm Bonner McGuire," the fellow said as he shook, "founder of this fine village." He smiled. "I'm the one as made the original discovery, you see."

"Gold?" Longarm asked.

"Aye. Free gold it is." Which Longarm knew meant gold that was not distributed within solid rock but that had been washed free of its original encasement. The precious metal was anything but "free" to take, considering the amount of labor required to pluck it out of the streams that carried it. "Would you be looking to purchase a claim now, Mr. Long?"

Longarm shook his head. "I should have explained. I'm a deputy United States marshal, and I need a horse and a gun. I'll pay for them, rent or purchase." He paused and added, "It's for official business."

McGuire fingered his beard for a moment before he spoke again. "I'll not be having either one o' those myself, you understand, but I might know someone who can help."

"I should tell you," Longarm said, "that I don't have much cash money on me. What I can do is give you a government voucher to be redeemed for cash."

"Oh, my. That does complicate things," McGuire said. Then he grinned. The expression had the effect of causing a row of yellowed teeth to appear in a bed of curly whiskers. "Nearly everyone in this camp owes me one sum or another. I could accept your scrip. How would that be?" The grin became wider. "Discounted by a certain small percentage."

"I think we can do business, Mr. McGuire," Longarm said, considerably relieved. For a moment he had feared he would have to walk back after those . . . whatever the hell they were. They were not robbers, exactly. But they *had* taken a prisoner away from Longarm's custody.

And that did most thoroughly piss him off.

"So let me tell you what I need," he said.

"Then let me tell you what I can provide," McGuire returned. "The two may differ, but between us we shall do as best we can."

Chapter 7

He had started a manhunt better equipped than this.

He had a dray horse, wide as a barrel and big as an ox, that did not object to having a human person on its back but which would only be plow-reined in order to change direction. As far as it was concerned, neck reining had not yet been invented.

McGuire had not been able to come up with any sort of saddle that would fit Pansy, so Longarm had to settle for a folded blanket and a rope around the body of the beast to hold the blanket more or less in place. He thought he might rename the animal Katie in honor of that barmaid he woke up next to back in Denver. Except that Katie probably weighed more than the horse. He decided to leave well enough alone and pretend that he did not know the dray was called Pansy.

In the way of armaments he had his own good derringer, an only slightly rusty cap-and-ball revolver that a down-on-his-luck miner was willing to part with, and a twelve-gauge double-barreled shotgun. He had ammunition for cach—not a lot but hopefully enough—that in the absence of saddlebags—and of course the absence of a saddle—he carried an ancient leather haversack slung over his shoulder by its one remaining strap. The bag looked like something that might have been carried in the Mexican-American War but it was sound enough and that was what mattered.

"Where can I find a hacksaw?" Longarm asked McGuire after he signed over a voucher for not more than three times the top dollar of what horse and gear should have been worth.

Henry would squawk at the size of the bill, but Longarm would rather argue with Henry than lose Charlie Cade.

McGuire nodded toward the north. "Second cabin over, other side of the road. He's our blacksmith hereabouts. Mends picks, fashions nails, whatever needs doing. If anyone in camp has a hacksaw, it'd be Gerald."

"And Gerald's last name would be . . . ?" Longarm asked.

McGuire chuckled. "You couldn't pronounce it. Trust me."

"Is this Gerald fella likely to be at the smithy at this hour or will he be wading in the creek?"

"Pretty sure he should be at the smithy. I saw smoke coming from the place when I passed by. Gerald, he doesn't like to leave a fire in the forge when he isn't there to see to things." McGuire laughed. "His first shed burnt to the ground one afternoon when he was letting some charcoal come ripe. Now he won't so much as step outside to piss when his forge is hot."

Longarm headed toward the door, stopped, and turned back. "You wouldn't happen to have a piece of cord, would you? Something I could use to sling this shotgun over my shoulder?"

"I got some primer cord. Would that do?"

"Uh . . . per'aps not. Got anything that won't blow my damn arm off?"

"Leather boot laces. How would those do?"

"That sounds just fine. How much d'you want for them?"

"For a good customer like you, I'll throw them in gratis."

"You're a gentleman and a scholar," Longarm said. The comment brought a huge belly laugh out of Bonner McGuire.

Longarm moved the haversack over to his left side, slung the shotgun on his right side, and figured that was as ready as he was likely to get. He nodded to McGuire, touched the brim of his Stetson, and headed outside.

He led the gray dray horse rather than bust his butt trying to mount the thing. He tied it to the iron ring attached to a hitching post outside the blacksmith's shop. Smoke still curled from a chimney on the side of the shed. Longarm stepped inside.

The smithy was past being warm. It was positively hot inside there. A very hairy man wearing a heavy cotton undershirt and a leather apron over canvas trousers was working with tongs, turning a piece of iron deep inside the glowing red coals in his furnace. The man had muscles that suggested he must have been hammering iron since he was a wee tyke. He looked up at Longarm's approach.

"You must be Gerald," Longarm said.

"That I be. And you?"

Longarm introduced himself. He offered his hand but took no offense when Gerald returned to his task—whatever the hell it was—rather than interrupt the heating process.

Gerald pointed with his chin and said, "Mind giving the bellows handle a couple pulls?"

"Don't mind at all, neighbor." Longarm stepped over to the handles of the huge, leather bellows and gave them a ride. The cherry red hunk of charcoal in the forge immediately flared.

"What can I do for you?" Gerald asked without stopping his work.

"I'm looking to borrow a hacksaw," Longarm told him.

"I need to cut the barrels down on this scattergun and then braise the rib back in place between them. I can make the cut myself but I'd have to ask you to finish the work afterward."

Gerald grunted. Longarm was not sure if that meant he would do the job or if he was suggesting that Longarm go fuck himself.

"Twenty-five cents," Gerald said. "You got cash money?"

"I can manage that much."

"Fine. Set down over there. I'll get to you when I'm done forming this hinge."

Longarm went in the direction indicated and settled onto a bench made from a good-sized aspen log split in two, with stout pegs bored into it to form the legs.

He laid the twelve-gauge over his lap and closed his eyes, willing to wait however long it took to accomplish what he wanted.

Chapter 8

The length of time Gerald required to form a simple hinge was a hell of a lot longer than Longarm would have thought. A competent smith could have formed that hinge and three more just like it in half the time this man took. But then under the circumstances a poor smith was better than none.

By the time Gerald had the barrels of the shotgun cut down to a length just forward of the splinter-style hand grip and the rib secured, it was coming dusk and Longarm's belly was beginning to growl.

"Is there a place around here where a man could get himself a meal?" he asked of the taciturn blacksmith.

Gerald pointed. "Last place on the left. Fellow there probably takes more dust outa the damn crick than any of us who pan for it. Hell, I make more off my smithing than I pan out of the crick."

"All right, thanks." Longarm paid the smith for his work, untied the big gray horse, and led it down to the café. Unlike most businesses in the camp, the café was housed under a huge tarp supported by poles and guy ropes. Half a dozen crudely built tables were behind the tent flaps that more or less kept road dust out. Once Longarm pushed past those, he found the place nearly empty. But then there was still a little daylight remaining, and the bulk of the community's population would still be out in the creek looking for gold.

The café was run by a skinny man who was tending a pair of collapsible sheet-metal sheepherder's stoves. His waiter was a boy who looked like he was not yet into his teens. Longarm guessed that would be the cook's son.

The kid rushed over to greet Longarm with "You want to eat, mister? One pinch of dust for a meal." He eyed Longarm's clothes and realized this was not a man who had just come out of the water. "Or twenty-five cents cash money, your choice."

"What's on your menu?" Longarm asked.

"Son of a bitch stew and coffee. Take it or don't, that's all we got."

"I'll take it," Longarm said. He chose a seat on a bench where he could watch the entrance—habit here, not necessity—and waited.

The boy plucked a tin bowl from a pile of them and ladled a generous portion of stew into it, then dipped a tin cup into a different pot and came up with steaming hot coffee. He carried the two to Longarm and set them down. "Two bits, mister."

Longarm paid the boy and asked, "You got a spoon I might use?"

The kid sniffed. "Most know to bring their own, but I expect we can loan you one." He went to a pan sitting on the ground close to the stoves and brought back a large spoon that looked like it was considerably older than the boy.

The spoon was dented and a little bent, but it appeared to be clean enough.

The stew smelled good, but Longarm knew better than to ask what was in it. His fear was that the kid might tell him. That could ruin what would otherwise be a good meal.

The stew tasted as good as it smelled. The coffee was black, hot, and stout enough to float nails.

By the time Longarm finished his meal, darkness had fallen beyond the light given off by four lanterns hanging from support poles, and the place was filling up with miners coming out of the stream. He would have stayed and relaxed with an after-dinner cheroot, but latecomers needed his place at the table. He picked up his shotgun and haversack and again draped them at his sides. He paused on his way out to light a cheroot from the flame in a lantern, then went out to the big gray horse that waited patiently outside.

It was already dark and he estimated it was a good six- or seven-hour ride back up the mountain to the spot where the stagecoach had been stopped.

Common sense suggested he should find a place to sleep and get a fresh start in the morning.

Longarm untied the gray and vaulted awkwardly onto its back.

He figured he could sleep when he got back to Denver.

Chapter 9

Longarm woke, sat up, and rubbed his eyes. He had reached the summit sometime short of dawn and lain down beside the road to catch a few winks while he waited for enough daylight to track the sons of bitches who stopped the stage and took his prisoner from him. Now the gray monstrosity was grazing peacefully nearby—without even bothering to look, Longarm could hear the grasses tear and the grinding of its teeth—its forelegs hobbled by the rope that had been used to tie its blanket in place, a blanket Longarm had appropriated to keep the chill of the night at bay.

There was no question that this was the right place. The chain brought out by the guard, thinking to use it to chain the off rear wheel, was lying coiled like a snake in the middle of the road.

Longarm stood up, stretched, and yawned hugely, then shivered. At this elevation a heavy coat would have been pleasant. Unfortunately both Longarm's sheepskin rancher-style coat and his army-style buffalo coat were back in Denver with his saddle, his Winchester, and a dozen other things he would have found useful here.

"You got anything to eat on you?" he asked Pansy, not really expecting an answer. After all, what did the horse have to worry about? It was standing in its breakfast. The gray dropped its head and tore out another mouthful of the sparse, high country grass.

Longarm shivered again and thought wistfully about the pint of rye whiskey he had . . . in his carpetbag, which he perforce had left back in that no-name mining camp. There was no way to carry the bag on Pansy in the absence of a saddle. That rye would have made a fine eye-opener on a cold morning. Just thinking about it, though, did nothing to warm his belly. He settled for turning to face the cutbank at the side of the road, unbuttoning his trousers, and taking a refreshing morning piss.

There was no earthly reason why he should turn away from the road to do that. No reason except habit.

Done, he tucked himself in and buttoned up again.

"Stay right where you are, horse, while I walk across the road an' see can I find us some tracks to follow. An' I'll look over that way first since it's just plain easier to go downhill instead of up. Make sense to you? I thought so. Have yourself another mouthful, why don't you."

Pansy dropped his head, he being a gelding despite the feminine name, and did help himself to that mouthful of grass.

Longarm strode across the roadway, his eyes on the ground looking for tracks.

"Right there," he said, loud enough for the horse to hear. "There's where the stage stopped. Just in front of where the chain lies. You can tell too from the footprints, see. These over here would be the coach line's shotgun messenger. He got down on this side. And over here are the fellows with the deep voice. These here would be Charlie's, and these little ones are where the woman got outa the coach.

They all o' them headed over to the downhill slope, just like I expected. Now let me walk over there an' see can a horse negotiate this hill or do I have to turn you loose to head on home while I walk from here. Don't go nowhere now."

Longarm sauntered across the road to the opposite side and took a look down the slope that lay on that side.

"Aw, shit!" he muttered. "Dammit all to hell."

Charles Cade's body was lying about fifty feet below the road grade. Even from where he stood Longarm could see that the man had damn near been cut in two by a shotgun blast fired at close range. The shotgun, presumably the one the stagecoach guard had relinquished to the highwaymen, lay tossed aside close by the body.

Longarm raised his eyes, his gaze sweeping across the grandeur of these mountains.

Somewhere out there, he knew, were the people who did this.

There was steel in Longarm's resolve when he started down toward what remained of Charles Cade.

Chapter 10

Longarm stood beside the mortal remains of Charles Cade.
Even for someone as accustomed to violence as a lawman
necessarily became, Cade's demise was an ugly one. Whoever shot the man must have used both barrels. The buckshot, fired at close range, opened Cade up like gutting a
fish. Coils of gray intestine spilled onto the ground beside
the body, and the gravel surrounding it was dark with dried
blood.

It was not, however, any of Custis Long's business. The
simple fact was that his assignment ended the moment
Charles Cade died, murder not being a federal crime. Now
the job of finding the killers and bringing them to justice
belonged to the local authorities, whoever they were, and
that would depend on whatever county this spot was in. That
might be Sheriff Jim Todd's Tillet County or perhaps the
jurisdiction adjacent.

The correct thing for Longarm to do now was to determine where he was in relation to county boundaries and
report the crime to the appropriate authorities, for them to
pursue.

He turned his head and spat. Like hell he was going to hand this off to someone else.

Locals would require at least another day, probably two, to come up here and start looking around. By then the trail would be days old. More than likely a cursory search would be conducted, after which everyone would go home and forget about Charlie Cade and his murder.

No damn way, Longarm growled softly to himself.

The bastards took his prisoner. Shoved a gun in his ribs and took Cade right out from under his nose. There was no way Custis Long would allow that to go unchallenged, jurisdiction be damned.

"Sorry, Charlie, I just don't have time t' get you planted proper," Longarm said aloud. "Maybe later sometime. For now, though, let's be putting you where the magpies an' the coyotes can't get to you."

He looked around for a likely spot then had to drag the corpse about forty yards to a wrinkle in the mountainside. He tucked Cade in there nice and snug and then spilled gravel and rock down on top of the body until it was completely covered. Without a shovel or a pick that was the best he could do.

He stuck an age-whitened length of dead pine where Cade's head would be, marking the spot for anyone who might want to come looking. And if no one ever did, well, there was no harm in that either.

Longarm was not one given to fancy words or high flying sentiments, but he did pause for a moment of respectful silence before he again draped the haversack and the sawed-off shotgun over his shoulders. He climbed back up to the road to collect the big gray and lead it carefully down the hillside. The horse snorted in fear and shied away when he led it past the spot where Cade was buried. Obviously the horse could smell death there, and if it could, then so would the coyotes. That was a shame, but there was nothing Longarm could do about it short of digging the man up again and taking him down to the mining camp where he got the gray.

That would mean virtually abandoning the hunt for the killers, and that he would not do.

No, these bastards belonged to him.

They just did not know it yet.

Chapter 11

Longarm climbed back up to the roadbed, retrieved the big gray beast, and walked along the shoulder of the road until he found a grade shallow enough for the horse to descend. He led it down to reasonably level ground, gathered the reins, and vaulted onto the gray's back. The shotgun hanging off his right shoulder swung around and gave him a painful whack in the lower back. He had had better days.

But then Charlie Cade had had better times than this too, so Longarm supposed he should consider his blessings before his difficulties.

He pulled the gray's head around to the right and started down the far side of the pass. He saw no tracks to follow, but it seemed only logical to head in that direction, as he had not seen the highwayman—and the bastard's female accomplice—on the other side of the pass. Roads being as scarce as they were in this country, they would pretty well have to have passed through the mining camp where Longarm found the gray horse, and he certainly had not seen them there.

The fold in the mountain that he was following re-

mained more or less level until it intersected with the public
highway. The middle of the road was of necessity full of
tracks from the passage of the stagecoach and other rigs,
but Longarm was interested in some hoofprints he found on
the fringe of the road.

At least two horses, he saw, possibly three. One print
was from something small, a barb perhaps or a large pony.
For the woman? He suspected so.

The tracks indicated that they were starting down where
the coach had climbed up. That made sense. They knew
Longarm was a deputy marshal. Surely they knew he would
not easily allow them to take his prisoner and kill the man.

Now they were . . . not running. The tracks suggested
horses moving at a walk. Could be that the woman was not
comfortable on horseback, he reasoned. Could be they were
slow because of her.

"Pansy, old boy," Longarm mumbled, "could be we've
drawn a high card for a change."

He nudged the big gray in the ribs and started down
the road.

Two hours on, the plodding gray rounded a curve and came
into view of a small settlement. Longarm did not remember
it from the uphill trip in the stagecoach, but then he had
been dozing through much of the journey.

This place was almost a mirror image of the community
where McGuire had outfitted him back on the other side of
the mountain.

Placer miners waded in a shallow creek, breaking their
backs and freezing their feet for a rare few flakes of gold.
Longarm knew that was damned hard work for damned
little return. After all, like almost everyone who came to
Colorado, he had tried it for himself. Hadn't liked it but he
had tried it.

He also knew why men abused themselves like this. The lure of striking it rich was a dream that was hard to discourage. Hit one really good pocket and a man could be set for life. Or at least for one good blowout. But generally speaking, a steady job shoveling horse shit in a livery barn would return more income. But that was not nearly so exciting, nor did it have the potential—however unlikely—that a placer claim or a dryland strike could provide.

He halted Pansy outside a tent with a hand-lettered sign out front that read "Salon." He suspected the writer intended to say "Saloon" . . . but then what the hell did he know? Could be it really was a salon.

Longarm threw a leg over the big horse's withers and slid to the ground, his knees just a little wobbly after several hours straddling that wide barrel. Even for a man who was accustomed to riding horseback since he was a boy, Pansy was more than a mite uncomfortable.

He tied the horse to an iron stake that secured one of the guy ropes on the front of the tent and pulled the front flap back so he could enter. He was pleased to discover that the place was indeed a saloon and not a salon.

Rough-hewn planks were laid across a pair of barrels to form a bar. The floor was dirt and gravel packed hard from the muddy boots of dozens of mining men. The backbar consisted of more planks and more barrels. A huge wooden tub held tin mugs jumbled in on top of one another, while several jugs, presumably holding homemade liquor, sat on the ground close by the tub. There were only five—he counted—actual whiskey bottles on the backbar plank, and Longarm would have waged a dollar to a dime that whatever was in those bottles never came from a bonded and tax-paid distillery.

A pair of immense beer barrels were sitting on makeshift supports, one fitted with a bung, the other with a tap.

He noticed the absence of any sort of free lunch. That extra was customary in more civilized parts, but not here. In fact he saw no sort of food anywhere in the place, not even a bowl of peanuts or parched corn. The whole outfit was rough and could easily be packed onto a single freight wagon and hauled away to the next gold strike, wherever that might be, when this stream was emptied of its gold.

There were no tables or chairs, but nine—he counted—empty kegs had been upended to serve the purpose. Those could be abandoned when the camp died as it inevitably must in a year, a month, a week, whenever.

There were seven—he counted—men in the place, four standing at the bar and three sitting on kegs they had pulled close enough for conversation. A barman who sported a huge mane of flaming red hair and a mustache to match stood behind the bar.

None of the men looked remotely like what Longarm would think his deep-throated highwayman should look like, all of them very obviously being working men in rumpled and dirty clothes. There were no women. Probably none in the camp. But he would have bet his last dime—the one he was sure he would have won on that wager about the whiskey bottles—that these boys would love to see even one fat, ugly, scabies-ridden whore come to take their gold dust away from them.

"Afternoon," he greeted, nodding, when the apron came to his end of the bar. "I'd take a beer if you please."

The redhead grunted by way of acknowledgment, plucked a mug out of the tub, and filled it at the tap. The man let the foam overflow onto the ground so the mug contained liquid and practically no head. Longarm appreciated that.

He laid a nickel on the plank. The barman gave him a hard glare and said, "You're halfway there, mister."

Longarm added a second nickel before he picked up his mug.

"Wonder if you could help me with something," he said.

"Maybe."

"I'm trying to find a young woman. We, uh, shared a coach for a spell and she, well, the truth is that I'd surely like t' see her again. I believe she came through here the other day, riding horseback with a man, could be more than one. Would you have seen them or know where I might could find them?"

"I don't pay no nevermind to what goes on past that canvas," the barman said, nodding toward the front wall of his tent, "but you can ask around. One of these boys that works outside might've noticed."

"All right, thanks." Longarm smiled and took a swallow of his beer. Which came very close to wiping the smile off his face. The stuff was sour. And flat. And tasted like shit. Well, not literally, but it was piss-poor beer. He smiled again and saluted the bartender with the mug. The cocksucker. Selling beer that bad should be a crime, and if it were, Longarm would have been pleased to arrest him for it.

"Yeah, thanks again." Longarm set the mug down and turned to talk with the other customers in the place.

Chapter 12

"No, mister, there's not a single damn woman in this camp, and more's the pity." The fellow dropped a shot into his beer and chugged down the result in one long gulp.

While the first gent was busy with his beverages, another piped up with "We had us a woman once. Cheap too. Oh, she was making out for a fortune except she turned belly-up an' died one day."

"Good thing too," someone else put in over that man's shoulder. "Bitch gave me the clap. Bunch of other boys too. We woulda strung her red ass up if she hadn't gone and died before we could."

"Served her right," a fourth man said. "I caught a dose from her too. Most everybody that was here then did."

"We haven't had a whore since," the first man said, running a hand over his mustache to wipe the suds away.

"And we sure as hell ain't seen a honest woman here. Not never."

"Poor thing wouldn't be safe if one was to come here," yet another put in, "though one might get away whole if she just rolled through on a stagecoach."

"But you haven't seen any strangers lately?" Longarm asked.

The first fellow shrugged and said, "What's a stranger anyway? This place didn't exist six months ago and likely won't exist six months from now. We're all of us strangers if it comes to that."

Longarm sighed. "You do have a point."

"We're being honest with you, mister. We ain't none of us seen anybody lately that didn't look like they either belonged here or ought to. For damn certain there's been nothing of the female persuasion here recent."

"All right, thanks." Longarm looked around the room and counted. The population had grown to nine now. He went over to the bar, laid a silver dollar on the plank and said, "Give everybody a beer on me, please, and have one for yourself."

The midday drinking crowd overheard and gave Longarm a chorus of cheers and thank-yous. He waved an acknowledgment and went back outside.

A cabin made of sapling sized-logs liberally chinked with crumbling mud was three places down. A sign posted in front of it said "Eats." Longarm untied Pansy and moved the big horse down to the café and around behind it.

He untied the rope that held his blanket in place on the gray's back, coiled it, and stuffed the rope into his haversack on top of his spare shotgun shells. He shook out the blanket and used his pocketknife to cut a four-inch-wide strip off the bottom, then used that material to hobble the horse's forefeet. He pulled the bridle and turned the gray loose to graze on the sparse grass available behind the café. The blanket he rolled and tied with the reins, then draped over his shoulder. Blanket roll, haversack, and shotgun . . . he was beginning to look like an infantryman preparing for a march. Not that he cared, he just found it mildly amusing.

The café was even more popular than the saloon at this hour in the working day. There must have been two dozen men gathered there—he did not bother to count them. A slate signboard offered a choice of porridge for ten cents or a full meal—the exact nature of that unspecified—for twenty-five.

Longarm found an empty place on a bench and staked it out for himself. A waiter wearing a once-white apron and a battered derby hat came to ask, "What's your preference, mate?" Longarm thought his accent was Australian, but he was not sure, and certainly was not interested enough to ask how someone from so far away would end up in this tiny corner of the world.

"I'll take the meal. What is it anyway?"

The waiter was gone before Longarm got the question out. He returned less than a minute later, and Longarm could find out for himself when the tin bowl was put before him along with a mug of coffee and a spoon.

Or not.

He peered into the bowl for some time but could not decide what he was about to eat. There was shredded meat that could have come from anything down to and including burro, along with rice, garlic, and onion. The consistency could as easily have been called a soup as a stew.

Whatever it was, it was hot and filling and not entirely unpleasant to the taste. Longarm finished his . . . whatever . . . and sat back with the coffee for a few minutes.

The loud buzz of chatter from the other diners flowed past unnoticed, nor did Longarm take note of the comings and goings of the men around him.

He mulled over the current situation while he sipped at the coffee. The woman and the highwayman were not here. He was fairly certain about that. They may or may not have passed through here on their way to . . . where?

And why had they killed Charlie Cade? That was the reason for the stickup. If one could call it that. They stole nothing from the mail, took nothing from the coach or the passengers. Except Cade.

His murder seemed to be the entire reason for their other actions. Logically then, Cade must have been a threat to them. Something Charlie Cade knew or something he had done endangered those two.

Or more. Longarm reminded himself that he did not really know how many there had been outside the coach that night. He knew there was at least one man out there. And the one woman inside the coach.

Cade's threat had to have been a serious one for them to risk taking him from federal custody and then commiting murder.

Murder would be prosecuted as a local matter, there being no federal statute against it, so the male was technically in the clear as far as Longarm was concerned. The woman, however, could be arrested under federal authority on a charge of assault on a federal employee, namely Deputy Marshal Custis Long.

He took a cheroot out of his coat, bit the twist off and spat it into his palm, then snapped a lucifer aflame. The first tasty draw on his smoke was in his mouth when he considered that he might not know what they feared from Cade but he did know *where*.

Cade was due to appear in court in Tillet County. He would have been prosecuted there. Would have given testimony there. The charges against him were . . . Longarm had to think back several days to what Henry had told him then . . . Assault? He thought that was what Henry said. Cade was to be tried for assault and battery. Longarm had not bothered to ask whom he assaulted. He certainly had not asked Cade why he assaulted someone. It was a county charge and as far as anyone in Denver knew strictly a Tillet County matter.

Until now.

The couple who took Cade from him seemed to have disappeared into thin air, but Longarm knew where he had been taking Cade, and he could reasonably assume that that was where the danger presented to the two by Charlie lay.

Longarm drank the last of his coffee and went outside to finish his smoke, then he walked out into a field of Indian paintbrush to gather up Pansy. He removed the hobbles, affixed the blanket in place again. and vaulted onto the big gray's back.

"Pansy old boy, we got us some traveling to do." Longarm nudged the horse in the sides to get him moving at his ponderous but steady pace.

He sawed back and forth on the reins to get lined out on the road back toward McGuire's place and beyond there to Buffington in Tillet County.

Chapter 13

"Hold up there." Longarm nudged Pansy out into the road to block the way, and the westbound stagecoach—the same route but a different driver from the one who had taken him the other day in the company of the late Charles Cade—came to a halt.

The driver threw up his hands and the guard threw down his shotgun, and Longarm called, "That was a poor choice of words, wasn't it? I didn't mean this is a holdup, boys, just that I wanted you t' hold the coach so's I can get aboard."

"Jesus, mister, you scared the shit outa us. You might not know it, but there was a holdup on this leg of the run just a few days back."

"Yeah, so I heard. How'd you find out about it?" Longarm asked as he stripped the blanket and bridle off Pansy's back. He slapped the big gray on the butt and turned it loose to find its own way home.

"Our driver wired the home office from Grand Junction. Said he didn't lose the mail though."

Longarm retrieved the guard's shotgun and handed it up to the man before climbing into the coach. There were only two passengers already inside, a pair of men wearing linen dusters and bored expressions. Longarm nodded and touched the brim of his Stetson, then settled into a corner and closed his eyes. He really was not in a mood for conversation.

Buffington, when he finally got there, was a more substantial town than he'd expected, it being a three-saloon community, featuring also a bank, two mercantiles, a gentleman's haberdashery, a dressmaker, a pharmacist, and a sprinkling of other businesses.

Just outside the town and arrayed along both banks of a broad, shallow creek were row upon row of fruit trees. Those trees, Longarm figured, were what would allow Buffington to survive long term, unlike the placer mining camps that disappeared as soon as the available gold dust was gone.

Longarm and one of the other passengers left the coach at the Buffington stop. He retrieved the carpetbag he had reclaimed from Bonner McGuire when the stagecoach passed through.

"I don't see a sign for a hotel hereabouts," he said to the Buffington manager, who was busy helping the stagecoach crew change out the team. "Where can a man put up for a few days?"

The local man seemed annoyed by the interruption, but he hooked a thumb toward the south end of town. "Boardinghouses. Follow your nose. You'll see."

"Thanks." Longarm picked up his things and headed in the direction the local fellow had indicated.

Just beyond the business blocks and before the orchards he saw several different houses with signs posted indicating they would welcome boarders. Longarm chose one that was small but tidy, let himself in through a gate in the picket fence, and mounted the steps onto a covered porch. He tapped on the door and took half a step back.

"Yes?" The door was opened by a middle-aged woman with her hair done up in a tight bun. She wore an apron over a drab brown dress. She also wore a very pleasant smile, which Longarm always thought was one of the nicest things a woman could have on.

He removed his hat and held it by his side. "Afternoon, ma'am. I'm looking to take a room for a few days."

"I'm sorry, sir. I don't take in short-term lodgers. You might try George Lewis. His house is the big one you see across the street there." She pointed. "Besides, I don't care for firearms." She eyed the shotgun that Longarm still had slung over his shoulder.

"I didn't know," Longarm said with a smile of his own. "I wanted to stay in your house because it's the best kept. I sure wouldn't want to distress you about the guns. Happens, though, that they're the tools o' my trade."

The lady's eyes widened. "What line of work are you in that you would say a thing like that?"

Longarm introduced himself and explained. He put the Stetson back on and nodded to the lady. As he started to turn and leave, she said, "Are you really a deputy marshal, Mr. Long?"

"Yes, ma'am."

"You have a badge and . . . everything?"

"Of course, ma'am."

"I think . . . Come inside, Marshal. I think I would like to have you lodge here while you are in town. And I think . . . I would like a chance to speak with you about . . . some things."

Longarm was puzzled, but the lady was not asking him for anything he could not willingly give. He took his hat off again and stepped forward. "At your convenience, ma'am."

Chapter 14

Longarm set his carpetbag in the room she gave him. The room, not surprisingly, was clean and pleasant. Much nicer, in fact, than the boardinghouse quarters he called home these days. He used his palm to press down on the mattress. It was firm and even seemed to be free of annoying lumps.

After the past few days he was dead tired and did not dare lie down yet. He was afraid he would not wake up for another two or three days if he did that, so all he did was to test the mattress, give the room a wistful glance, and go back to the parlor, where his temporary landlady—she gave her name as Georgia Cooper—was busy cleaning the floor with an odd-looking suction device.

"You wanted to talk to me, ma'am?" he asked.

"Why, yes, I . . . I do, Mr. Long. But . . . I need to gather my thoughts. Would you mind? After dinner, perhaps?" He got the impression that she was a little flustered.

In fairness, he had pretty much sprung himself on the lady. She would have had no way of knowing a federal peace officer would be asking for one of her rooms, so if

Mrs. Cooper needed to collect her thoughts—or her nerve—
it was no surprise.

"That'll be fine, ma'am."

"Thank you, Mr. Long. Have you a watch?"

"Yes, ma'am."

"Dinner will be at six-thirty. Will that be all right with
you?"

He judged the time now to be somewhere in the neighborhood of half past two. "Just fine, ma'am. I'll try and be
on time."

The lady nodded and smiled and went back to cranking
her suction machine. Longarm thought she could achieve
the same result with less effort if she just used a broom. But
then what the hell did he know about housekeeping? He
smiled back at her, put his Stetson on, and stepped out onto
the porch. What he needed now was direction to Sheriff Jim
Todd's office.

"Shit." Longarm rattled the doorknob and knocked on the
glass, harder this time, but there was no response from inside the courthouse office, nor could he see any movement
in there when he looked as best he could through the frosted
glass panels.

He would have thought a county officer would at least
hang a sign or post a note on the door saying when he expected to return, but not Todd. Dammit! Longarm turned
away, looked up and down the corridor without seeing any
life, and went back outside.

There was a café across the street. He assumed that was
where the public employees would take their breaks. It could
even be that he would find the sheriff there. He hustled down
the marble steps of the small but very handsome Tillet County
courthouse, walked past the benches set along the rim of
the public square, and crossed over to Martha's Café.

"Martha" turned out to be a hairy man with a five-day beard stubble and jowls that would make a boar hog jealous. Martha's Café had a dozen patrons or more, all of them dressed like city folk.

Longarm chose a stool at the counter, tucked in between two gents with the arrogant look of public servants. Before he could speak to either of his seatmates, the cook came to take his order.

"Coffee, I reckon. An' since I've never been here before, would you mind if I ask a question?"

"You can ask," the fellow said. "Whether I answer or not depends on the question."

"I'm wondering, is there an actual Martha what owns this place?"

The man laughed. So did several of the patrons nearby. "I'm Martha," the fellow said. And laughed again. "John Martha, at your service."

"Mr. Martha, you put my mind at ease 'bout that. Thank you. I'd like to ask you somethin' else as well. I'm looking to see the sheriff. Fella name of Todd, I believe. I stopped over at the courthouse, but the sheriff's office is locked an' empty. Would you or any of the rest of you fellows know where I can find Sheriff Todd?"

"Finding him is easy enough," the man on Longarm's right said, "but he won't talk to you if you do."

"What makes you say that he wouldn't talk to me?"

The man grunted. "Because we buried Jim yesterday. Some son of a bitch shot him dead."

Longarm pushed his Stetson back on his head and reached for the coffee that John Martha had set in front of him. "That do make things difficult, don't it," he mused. "So what are you folks doing for your local law?"

The gent on Longarm's left side said, "We have a town marshal."

"Useful as tits on a hound," Martha put in.

"You shouldn't speak about Gaddis that way, John. He does the best he knows how."

"Yes, and he doesn't know shit about much of anything," Martha said.

"He tries," the man on the right said. "He tries."

"Yes. He tries," Martha agreed. He looked at Longarm and shrugged his massive shoulders. "Sorry, friend. We really shouldn't vent our troubles on you."

The fellow on the left touched Longarm's forearm and said, "Will Gaddis has an office . . . sort of an office . . . next door to Gaylord's Saloon. Look for him there if you want to see him now that Jim is gone."

"All right, thanks." Longarm dropped a nickel on the counter to pay for his coffee, then rose and headed out the door without pausing to taste it. Damn but it did smell good, though.

Chapter 15

Gaylord's was in the middle of the next block over. Finding it was easy enough as there was a large sign that ran the length of the false front, atop the single-story building that housed the saloon. Beside it on one side was a gentleman's haberdashery. On the other was what looked to be an empty storefront. If it was the office for Buffington's town marshal, they were hiding the fact awfully well, Longarm thought.

Those fellows had said to look in Gaylord's. Probably they knew what they were talking about. With a shrug and a shake of his head, Longarm headed for the saloon.

Gaylord's was the sort of place where a man could find comfort and an escape from the annoyances of life. It was pleasantly dark, illuminated only by the light coming in through a pair of windows that flanked the open doorway.

Laid out shotgun style, running narrow but deep, the room housed a bar stretched almost the entire depth of the building on the left, while small tables and chairs were scattered along the right-hand wall. There were no whores visible, no gaming tables, not even billiards. Gaylord's was a place where men could come for quiet conversation and drinks. At the moment a score or more customers were in the place, most of them holding down the foot rail in front of the bar.

Longarm approached the bar and tipped his Stetson back. "Afternoon," he said to the bartender, a bald man with a florid complexion.

"Welcome," the fellow said, wiping his hands on a towel. The bar towel looked clean, a small sign that the place was probably very well run. "What can I get you?"

"Beer, please."

"Coming right up."

When the barman returned to set a foamy mug in front of Longarm, Custis asked, "Where can I find your marshal? Fellow name of Gaddis, I'm told."

The bartender accepted Longarm's nickel and inclined his head to his left. "Next to the last gentleman at the end of the bar there."

"Thank you, sir." Longarm picked up his mug and carried it down the bar to the man who'd been pointed out to him.

Will Gaddis looked to be a man in his sixties or even seventies. He had snowy white hair that was overdue for cutting and a mustache that hung down over his mouth. It was coated with foam off the top of his beer.

He had leathery age- and weather-cracked skin and pale, rheumy eyes with dark circles permanently etched beneath them. He was wearing a suit coat that was probably older than Longarm, striped trousers, and low quarter shoes. If he was carrying any sort of weapon, he was hiding it well. He had a chromium-plated star pinned prominently on his lapel.

"Howdy," Longarm said.

The marshal glanced at him, looked away, and raised his mug to dunk his mustache in the suds again.

"I said hello," Longarm insisted.

Gaddis looked his way again. It was obvious he was annoyed by this interruption of his drinking.

"You are the town marshal, aren't you?"

The man grudgingly nodded.

"I want to report a crime."

"Where'd it happen?" His voice held no real interest in the question.

"Up on top o' Fike's Summit," Longarm said, repeating the name McGuire had given him when he reclaimed his carpetbag.

Gaddis grunted. "Not my affair," he said. "Out of my jurisdiction."

"You're the only law in these parts until someone takes over as sheriff," Longarm said.

"I'm *town* marshal. You wouldn't know how the law works, but there is a difference between the town and the county. It isn't all the same thing."

"Matter of fact I do know a little bit about how the law works," Longarm said, "and one thing I know is that you could take an interest in this if you want to."

"That right there answers the question for you, mister," Gaddis said. "I don't want to. Now, please leave me be." Gaddis turned his back, picked up his beer, and moved down to the very end of the bar.

So much for trying to be polite, Longarm thought. He tasted his own beer. It was fresh, with a bright, crisp flavor.

He licked the foam off his mustache and wondered what the hell he should do now.

Chapter 16

Supper, he decided. That was the thing he should do next. Have something to eat, get some sleep—the past several nights had not been conducive to rest, being spent either bouncing around inside a stagecoach or lying down on hard ground without benefit of so much as a bedroll—and let his mind chew on the question of where to go next. He had long since found that if he slept on a problem the solution would present itself when he woke up.

Or not.

It was worth a try anyway.

He had one more of Gaylord's good beers, gave the barman a nod of thanks, and ambled down the street to Mrs. Cooper's house.

"You're early for dinner, Marshal," the lady said when he let himself in and hung his Stetson on a hat rack beside the front door. "Would you like a glass of wine while you wait?"

"No, ma'am, but I could sure use some coffee if you have some."

"Of course. Sit down wherever you like. I'll bring it to you."

She turned toward the kitchen, but he stopped her with a question. "Do you allow smoking in the house, ma'am?"

"No, I do not, Mr. Long."

"Then if it's all the same to you, I'll take my coffee on the porch."

"That will be fine." She smiled—he really did like her smile, it almost made this plain woman seem rather pretty—and once more headed toward the back of the house.

Longarm retrieved his hat and put it on, then went out onto the porch. There were four rocking chairs out there. He chose the one at the far right end of the porch so he could flick his cigar ashes into the flower bed below the porch floor and not make a mess that Mrs. Cooper would have to sweep up after him.

He took his time about trimming off the twist and lighting the dark, slim cheroot. By the time his cigar had a good coal building on the tip, Mrs. Cooper had come out with his coffee.

She handed the cup to him but instead of returning inside her house she drew another rocker close and sat down.

Recalling what the lady had said earlier, Longarm said, "This afternoon you told me there was something you wanted to talk about."

"Yes, if . . . Marshal, there is probably nothing you can do about this. I know no federal crimes have been committed."

He raised an eyebrow. "But . . . ?"

"But I have a problem." She looked away. "I may well lose my home."

"That'd be terrible, ma'am. How come you say that?"

"There is someone," she looked at him, then dropped her eyes, wringing her hands and swallowing hard several times before she went on. "There is someone who says he has a quit-claim deed. He says my husband lost the house in a poker game." She looked up, her expression bleak. "He says he intends to file papers in the courthouse to have me evicted."

"The first question, ma'am, is did your husband lose the house?"

Again she looked away. "I . . . I don't know."

"You haven't asked him?" Longarm took a drag on his cheroot and sat for a moment while Mrs. Cooper agonized over what should have been a simple enough question.

Without looking at Longarm again, she said, "I haven't seen John, not to speak to that is, for more than a year. I still see him on the streets sometimes, but . . . I believe I am what is called a grass widow. Certainly the whole town regards me as a widow. Everyone knows."

"So d'you think your husband really did lose the place like that fella said?"

She began knotting her apron, her hands clutching and twisting the cloth. Longarm doubted she even knew she was doing it. "He might have signed it over," she conceded, "but he had no right to do such a thing. The deed is recorded in my name. I . . . I think."

Mrs. Cooper looked up and made eye contact with him again. "What should I do, Marshal? Who can I turn to?"

"Well, for sure your town marshal won't look into it," Longarm said. "Look, um, tomorrow I'll be going over to the courthouse anyway. I'll ask the clerk there about your house."

Her smile returned in full force. "Thank you, Marshal. Thank you very much."

"Yes'm." Longarm smiled back at her and took another drag on his cheroot.

"I will have supper on the table in a jiffy," the lady said, letting go of her now very rumpled apron and rising from the rocking chair.

"I'll be right in," he said, "soon as I finish this smoke."

He wondered briefly where the other boarders were. Surely they would know when supper was to be served.

Not that it was any of his business. He rocked back and sat for a moment admiring the length of firm ash on the tip of his cigar before reaching out and tapping the ash into the flower bed cultivated beside the porch. Fertilizer, he thought. Good for the plants.

"Supper is ready," he heard from inside the house. He stood, tossed what was left of his cheroot into the bushes, and went inside.

Chapter 17

Longarm rose from the table and laid his napkin beside his plate. "Fine meal, ma'am. Thank you."

"It is my pleasure to cook for such a nice gentleman as yourself, Marshal." There was that smile again. Mrs. Cooper began clearing the dishes away. "Why don't you sit on the porch and have a cigar while I take care of these things," she said. "Then if you don't mind I'd like to close up and go to bed early." The smile. Again even broader. "You know the old saying, 'Early to bed and early to rise makes a man healthy, wealthy, and wise.'"

"I got the healthy part covered," Longarm responded. "Don't know about the wise though, an' I dam— uh, darn sure missed out on the wealthy stuff."

Mrs. Cooper chuckled and disappeared into the kitchen with an armload of their supper dishes.

Longarm shook his head. Damnedest boardinghouse he ever saw. She was going to turn him down, yet there were no other boarders. At the table it had been only he and the lady. No one else at all.

On the other hand, Mrs. Cooper could damn sure cook.

That was as fine a meal as he'd had in many a day.

He fingered his pockets, then went to his bedroom and retrieved some cheroots and a fresh supply of matches from his carpetbag. He also took an after-dinner nip from the flask of Maryland distilled rye whiskey that he carried for emergencies. This was not an emergency, exactly, but the rye tasted mellow and warm going down anyway.

He wandered out onto the porch, again chose the rocking chair on the far right and settled in to enjoy the evening air. Buffington's elevation was low enough that the air was soft and pleasantly cool, without the cold bite in it that one felt in the mountains.

He was on his second cigar and thinking about that flask of rye whiskey when Mrs. Cooper came out carrying a small, silver tray with two short, rounded glasses and a cut glass decanter.

"I thought you might join me in a glass of brandy, Marshal. Please do, as a lady should not drink alone and I seldom have such pleasant company."

"If you put it that way, ma'am, I reckon I could stand a little brandy." Brandy was not Longarm's favorite tipple, but he could stand it when need be. It sure as hell beat the wine she'd mentioned before. The way he saw it, wine was good for washing horses' hooves but not much more.

Mrs. Cooper again sat next to him. Quite close to him in fact. She poured a snifter of brandy for him and another for herself.

The brandy was not too bad, if a little fruity for Longarm's taste. It did warm a man's belly almost as nicely as whiskey did.

When they were on their second glasses, with crickets chirring in the night, Mrs. Cooper set her glass down and said, "May I ask you something, Marshal?"

"Of course."

"Do you find me to be an attractive woman?"

The question was a surprise, to put it mildly. He said, "Why yes, ma'am. You're a handsome woman indeed." And would have been even better looking after a few more brandies, he thought but did *not* say aloud.

"Not too old?"

"No, ma'am, not at all."

"Then may I ask for a favor?"

"Of course, ma'am."

"Would you sleep with me tonight? Please?"

Longarm's head snapped around toward her. He could barely see her in the darkness, with only a faint glow of lamplight sneaking out from behind the curtains in the lady's front window. He could see enough, though, to tell that she was smiling at him again.

"I, uh, I . . . Why yes, ma'am. I'd be honored."

"Thank you, Marshal."

He coughed into his fist and said, "Under the circumstances, ma'am, I expect you could call me Longarm instead of Marshal. That's what I'm generally known by."

The lady laughed and said, "Let's go inside now, Longarm. I'm getting *very* tired and I want to go to bed."

Chapter 18

"How old are you?" Longarm blurted the question before he had time to think. Or to put a rein on his tongue.

Mrs. Cooper stopped in the midst of removing a stocking and looked at him, then laughed. "I am fifty-three years old," she said. Said it rather proudly actually.

"Damn good-looking fifty-three," Longarm responded. He smiled and added, "Damn tidy figure." He meant it.

Georgia Cooper was smaller beneath the layers and ruffles of her undergarments than he would have expected. She had slim legs, the flesh loose and beginning to wrinkle, but slim nonetheless.

She was sitting on the side of her canopied bed. She tossed the cotton stocking aside. Wearing only a bustier and pantaloons, she walked to the mirrored dressing table and reached up to unpin her hair, then with a shake of her head sent it cascading down around her shoulders. Her hair was mostly gray but not unattractive.

She returned to stand before Longarm. Looking him in the face, she untied the waist string of her pantaloons and wriggled out of them, dropping them to the floor in a heap of pale ruffles. Her pussy hair was entirely gray and not very thick. He could see moist, pink flesh not quite hidden inside the bush.

Mrs. Cooper smiled. And began unbuttoning the bustier. Slowly. Teasing him. And enjoying it.

That seemed fair enough. Longarm was enjoying it too.

"Nice," he said when her breasts finally were revealed.

Her tits were large, set on a very small frame, the nipples as thick as his thumbs, long and red and erect. She cupped one breast in the palm of each hand and offered them to him.

Longarm took the woman into his arms and kissed her, then guided her to the bed, where he sat and she stood, putting his face on a level with her tits. He took one engorged nipple into his mouth, swishing it around with his tongue and sucking on it. Then he repeated the process with her other nipple.

Her tits sagged, which was to be expected with a woman her age, and they were pale, red veins showing through a thin covering of skin. They seemed to have lost none of their sensitivity, though, as she began to moan and her hips to writhe as he suckled.

She took one of his hands and pushed it down, making it clear what she wanted him to do.

Longarm obliged, his fingers finding her pussy and sliding inside.

Mrs. Cooper stiffened. She gulped a sharp intake of breath and began running a hand over the back of his head and neck while still he sucked one nipple and then the other.

"Teeth," she whispered. "Use your teeth."

He complied, but carefully so he did not damage her.

"Harder," she demanded. "Yes. Harder. Harder. *Oh!*" The last came out as a cry. For a moment he thought he had gone too far and hurt her left nipple. Then he felt the fluttering contractions of her pussy clenching tight on the fingers that were inside her and he realized that she had reached a climax from the combination of sensations at nipple and pussy.

She grabbed the back of his head and yanked him hard against her left tit, cutting off his breath and damn near smothering him with soft flesh. Longarm managed to turn his head and gulp in some air. She was still shuddering from the force of her climax.

After a few moments she let him go and took a step backward. She smiled at him.

"Now it's your turn," she said. "Get those clothes off and lie down. I want you to just lie there on your back. I will do the rest and . . . I think you will be pleased."

As indeed he was.

Very pleased.

Chapter 19

Longarm woke in his own room. He had left Georgia Cooper's canopy bed sometime . . . He did not know exactly when, but probably closer to dawn than to midnight. He yawned and stretched. Felt pretty damned good if the truth be known. But then it always seems to give a man a sense of well-being when his balls are so thoroughly emptied.

He had to give the woman credit. Georgia could really drain a man's sap. Mouth, cunt, or asshole, she did not just passively take, she aggressively attacked, and seemed to receive as much pleasure as she gave. And she gave considerable. Longarm smiled, remembering.

After a few moments he rolled out of bed and dressed. He walked softly so as to avoid waking Georgia, only to find that she was already up and had biscuits in the oven.

"Coffee?" she asked.

"Oh, yes."

She poured a cup for him and said, "Sit down. I'll have your breakfast on the table in a minute." Her fingertips brushed lightly across the back of his neck when a few minutes later she leaned over him to set his breakfast in front of him.

"What do you plan today?" she asked.

Longarm shrugged. "No plan, exactly. First thing, I need to have me a shave. It's been a while."

She smiled—Lordy but she did have a fine smile—and said, "You are more than a little scratchy. The insides of my thighs are bright red this morning from where your beard . . . you know."

"Yeah, but you didn't seem to mind it all that much last night."

"I am not complaining, sir. More like bragging. That is a lovely place to get whisker burn." She laughed and began tending to her stove, using a folded cloth to keep from burning her fingers when she opened the firebox and shoveled two chunks of pine in.

Longarm finished his meal and went back to his room to retrieve his coat. He paused to light a cheroot, then went outside to greet a fine, bright morning.

Walking into town, he first looked for a hardware and then, even better, spotted a gun shop almost hidden on a side street. He was not sure he would be willing to trust his life to the cap-and-ball relic with its barrel sticking out of his holster at the moment. It had been the only thing available back there in the mountains, but Buffington was a different proposition. Here there were proper amenities to be had.

"Good morning, sir. How can I help you?" the proprietor said in greet.

Longarm laid the near antique on the counter and said, "I want a replacement for this. Something double-action if possible, .45-caliber, short barrel."

"The short barrel I have, but double-action . . . ?" The fellow shook his head.

"The barrel length is more important," Longarm conceded. "Something that'll come outa this holster nice an' quick."

"I have just the thing here." The man reached beneath the counter and brought out a .45-caliber Colt.

"I'll take it," Longarm said after a brief inspection. The gun was used but in good condition. "And a box o' twelve-gauge buckshot too."

Five minutes later Longarm walked out feeling properly armed.

He stopped to take a seat on one of the park benches in front of the Tillet County courthouse, then after a few minutes hustled up the marble steps and interrupted a county clerk's perusal of a newspaper. Longarm recognized the man as one of the coffee coolers he'd seen in John Martha's café the day before.

"Who is in charge of law enforcement in Tillet County now that your sheriff is dead?" he asked the white-haired gentleman.

"Oh, I suppose Judge Lawson would be the one you want for that," the clerk answered.

"And where might I find him?"

"Upstairs," the clerk said with an upward sweep of his chin to point out where upstairs might be. "His office is right next to the courtroom. You can't miss it."

"All right, thanks. And while I'm here, I'd like to see the deed for a house over yonder." Longarm pointed. "I'm not sure what the street address would be, but the one I'm interested in is owned by a Mrs. Georgia Cooper."

"My oh my," the clerk said as he turned toward the shelf of large, gray canvas-covered record books. "That's the second request I've had for that this month. Is there something going on with that property that I should know about?"

"Now, ain't that interesting," Longarm said. "Why don't you tell me about the other request."

"Oh, I'm not sure I should do that, sir."

Longarm took his wallet out of his coat pocket and laid it open with his badge showing.

Not that he had an iota of authority in Tillet County, which the clerk would realize if he stopped to think about it.

"As you say, Marshal," the clerk said quickly. He placed the heavy record book on the counter, opened it, leaned forward, and then began to speak.

Chapter 20

Longarm went back to Georgia Cooper's boardinghouse to deposit the box of shotgun shells in his carpetbag. Georgia was outside tending her flower beds, so he greeted her formally and refrained from playing grab-ass games with the woman. But he did get one of her delightful smiles, and that had to be considered a plus.

On his way back out he tipped his hat to her and gave her a wink and a cockeyed grin. After that last night he was definitely looking forward to more. Later.

"Good day, ma'am."

"Good day, Marshal."

From the boardinghouse he headed back into town, admiring the fruit orchards along the way. When he got back to the courthouse square, he stopped at Martha's Café. It was again doing a brisk trade.

Longarm took a stool at the counter. John Martha greeted him and said, "You must have liked us well enough yesterday, as I see you've come back. What will it be for you this morning?"

"Just coffee. I've already had somethin' to eat."

Martha set a cup down and poured coffee into it. In truth it tasted better than Georgia's.

"Can I ask you something, please?"

"Sure. Whatever you like," the café owner said.

"What do you do with all the fruit you grow around here? Surely there isn't enough of a market locally." He smiled. "Not unless you all set around an' eat fruit day an' night."

"Oh, no. We box it and cart it down into New Mexico Territory. There's a good market for fresh produce of any sort in Taos and Santa Fe and like that. Easier for us to get to than across to Pueblo or Colorado City, you see. Besides growing the fruit, we have a mill that makes boxes to ship the fruit in." Martha laughed. "We don't have all that much of a population, so around picking time we're busier than a one-armed juggler. The rest of the time, though, we go pretty easy."

"Thanks. I was curious about that. I—"

"*You!*"

Longarm was interrupted by a shout at the front door. A very angry shout.

He turned to see a dark-haired stranger pointing at him. "You're the son of a bitch who's messing in my affairs."

"I am *what*?" Longarm snapped back at him. He swiveled around on the stool. Men on either side of him melted away toward the walls, while John Martha moved quickly to the far end of his counter.

"You heard me, damn you."

"Mister, you must have one hellacious set of balls on you if you think you can come in here and talk to a perfect stranger like that. Now you'd best back off an' do it real fast."

"They told me at the courthouse that you were nosing around for the deed to my property."

The newcomer was whip thin with a fancy trimmed goatee

and long sideburns. He wore a narrow-brim hat pulled low over his eyes and a brace of pistols in a shoulder harness, clearly visible because his coat was pulled back out of the way, presumably to let him get at the guns just a little quicker.

He advanced menacingly across the room to stand glowering in front of Longarm, who rose to his feet at the man's approach.

"I don't stand for anyone messing in my affairs," the fellow declared.

"That's interesting," Longarm said mildly.

"I just may decide to kill you," the fellow snarled.

"That'd be up t' you," Longarm told him.

"Draw!"

"Fuck you," Longarm snapped.

"I said draw."

"I heard you the first time."

"Damn you."

Longarm reached for a cheroot. With his left hand. His antagonist, whoever the son of a bitch was, decided to draw himself if Longarm would not. His right hand shot across his body for the pistol beneath his left arm.

Longarm palmed his own Colt.

And whacked the fellow on his left ear—hard—while Longarm's left hand was clamped around the man's right wrist—hard—stopping him from reaching the revolver in that shoulder holster.

"Ow!" His howl could likely be heard two blocks away. "That hurt, dammit."

"Ayuh, I would expect that it did. It was s'posed to. Now either sit down and state your business plain or get the hell outa here." Longarm glared down at him from a height advantage of a good five inches. "And don't even think about reaching for those shooters again. Next time I'll save myself and everybody else in this town some trouble and put a bullet between your eyes."

Longarm turned half away from the man—but only half, as he wanted to keep the fellow in his peripheral vision—and picked up his coffee cup. "I could use a refill here, John."

The gent with the bad attitude stamped his foot once, turned, and headed for the door at a gait just barely shy of a run.

Chapter 21

Longarm looked up in time to see John Martha trying, with fair success, to stifle a laugh.

"Something wrong?" Longarm asked.

"No, no, nothing's wrong. It's just that I've never seen Wilson back down before. He tends to ride roughshod over us locals."

"Wilson," Longarm repeated. "What's the rest of his name?"

"Anthony G. Wilson. I don't know what the G stands for."

"Everyone call him Tony?" Longarm asked.

"Not unless you're looking for a gunfight," Martha said. "He prefers Mr. Wilson, but he'll answer to Anthony. But *never* call him Tony."

Longarm grinned, and Martha said, "Why is it that I think the next time you see the man you will be calling him Tony?"

The grin turned into a laugh. "You must be right good at guessing games, John."

"Normally I would suggest that you watch yourself, but I get the impression that you can take care of yourself mighty well."

"Is that a plate o' sinkers I see on the shelf there?"

"Made fresh this morning."

"Let me have one of 'em then, please. Mr. Wilson seems to have whetted my appetite."

Longarm broke the doughnut in half and dunked the pieces in his coffee. He enjoyed both, then dropped a quarter on the counter, tipped his hat to Martha, and ambled down the street toward where he recalled seeing a red and white striped barber pole.

He was the only customer in the place when he entered. The barber, a thin man with a forehead that extended halfway toward the back of his head, jumped out of his barber chair and reached for a sheet. "You're next, sir."

Longarm placed his Stetson on the rack beside the door, shucked off his coat and hung that too, then unbuckled his gunbelt and hung that beside the coat. He loosened his string tie and removed his collar stud.

"I can take those for you, sir," the barber said.

Longarm handed them over and settled into the chair. The barber snapped the sheet a few times and let it float down over Longarm's clothing. He wrapped it tight around Longarm's neck and pinned it in place, then tucked a tissue under the collar.

"Shave and a haircut, sir?"

"Just the shave, please. An' leave the mustache be. I'll do that my own self."

"As you wish, sir." The gent got his soap and brush and started whipping up a lather. "New in town, sir?"

"Ayuh. Got in just yesterday."

"I think you will find us to be a friendly community."

"Oh, I'm sure I will," Longarm drawled, deadpan. He was thinking, though, about the welcome Anthony G. Wilson already gave him.

The barber took a moist towel out of a warming oven

and placed it over Longarm's face. "Too hot, sir?"

"Just fine," Longarm said.

The bell suspended over the front door jingled. Longarm lifted his head a little so he could see who had come in.

It was Anthony G. Wilson.

"Why, hello, Tony."

"You called me that deliberate, didn't you?" Wilson snarled. He swiveled his head to the left, toward the hat rack where Longarm's hat and coat . . . and gunbelt . . . were hanging.

"Yes, Tony, indeed I did. I hear you don't like to be called that. Bigger kids used t' call you that, did they? Beat you up, maybe?"

"Why don't you go look for something you forgot in the back room, Sydney."

"I . . . I don't want to get involved in this, Mr. Wilson."

"Oh, I'm sure you don't. Go on now."

"Nothing is going to happen here, Sydney," Longarm put in, his eyes locked on Wilson's. "Tony here doesn't have the nerve to find out what I'm holding in my hand underneath this sheet."

"You're bluffing," Wilson said. "I know damned good and well you're bluffing."

Longarm grinned. "All right. Call my bluff. *If* I'm bluffing."

"I . . . I would. Of course. If I came here to do anything. I just wanted . . . wanted to make you sweat a little."

"You're a liar," Longarm said calmly, "and a coward. Can I say it any plainer for you, Tony? You're both a liar and a coward, and everybody in this town is gonna know it because I intend to tell them."

"Damn you," Wilson blurted. "I ought to kill you." He began to tremble.

"You see my gun hanging over there, Tony. Hell, it isn't

even my regular gun. I've never had a chance to fire this one. Not that that matters, since I can't reach it anyhow. So d'you feel this is your lucky day? D'you want t' call my bluff . . . if it's a bluff?"

"I just came in here to warn you to stay out of my way," Wilson said.

"Why, thank you, Tony. That's real sporting of you. Now run along. Maybe you can find a woman to beat up on. That should be about your style. Go on, Tony. Shoo!" Longarm's left hand came out from under the sheet and he made a sweeping motion as if to brush Wilson out of his way.

Wilson turned bright red, but he whirled around and practically ran out of the barbershop onto the street.

"That was some bluff," Sydney said.

Longarm winked at him. "'Twasn't a bluff."

But his .41-caliber derringer was out of sight in his vest pocket again when the sheet came off.

Chapter 22

Longarm felt better after his shave. Smelled pretty damn good too. He was not sure just which astringent Sydney used after shaving him, but he liked it. A little more interesting than the ordinary bay rum but not flowery. He definitely did not like a flowery aftershave.

He buckled his gunbelt around his waist, took his hat and coat down from the rack, and considered himself fit to meet Tillet County's judge. But if this kept up, he was going to be thought of as one of the regulars at the courthouse. On his way up the steps to the main door, he passed the elderly clerk he had spoken with earlier. The fellow was more than likely heading for Martha's Café for his morning coffee. Longarm tipped his hat to the gentleman and kept on going.

Upstairs, the clerk had said, next to the courtroom.

It would have been difficult to miss it. There was a frosted glass pane in the door, very carefully lettered with "Judge Albert Hamm Lawson."

Longarm was not sure if he should knock to gain entry or if there was an outer office with a secretary so he should simply go in to make himself known. He decided to knock. Never offend a judge, never, even if the man is only a county judge.

"Come," he heard from the other side of the door.

He pulled the door open and entered a very small office in which a young man in sleeve garters, open collar, and bulky cuff protectors was seated behind a desk that was littered with papers. The young fellow looked up at the interruption. "Can I help you?"

"I'd like to see the judge."

"What about?"

Longarm pulled out his wallet and opened it to display his badge. "Deputy U.S. Marshal Custis Long," he said, "and I have some questions about a case that was to be brought here."

"What would you like to know?" the young man asked, leaning back from the pile of work on his desk and giving his attention to the visitor.

"Look, if you don't mind," Longarm said, "I'd really like to see the judge."

The fellow laughed and said, "And so you are."

"Pardon me?"

"I am Judge Lawson." He stood and extended his hand to shake. "It's a pleasure to meet you, Deputy. Sit down." He pointed to a straight-back wooden chair in the corner. "What would you like to talk about?"

Longarm sat, still surprised that this young fellow who looked like he could scarcely be out of his teens was the county judge. Lawson was blond, which probably contributed to his youthful appearance, and he had no facial hair. At first glance he looked like he was not old enough to grow any, but that was probably untrue. It was just that his smooth skin and bright blue eyes gave that impression.

"Normally," Longarm said, "I'd not bother you but talk

with your sheriff instead, but yesterday I found out that Sheriff Todd was killed."

"Yes. He was murdered," Lawson said, "shot in the back through an open window while he was eating his supper. The assassin is unknown."

"D'you know why he was killed?" Longarm asked.

"I have no idea," the judge said. "I wish I did. I would personally swear in a posse comitatus and lead them to arrest the son of a bitch."

"It's a shame I can't help," Longarm said, "though I'd be glad to if you can think of any way that'd be possible."

"Thank you. Is that why you came by this morning?" The judge leaned forward in his chair and fingered some of the papers on his desk, suggesting he wanted to get back to his work.

"No, sir. Actually I'm wantin' to find out what you know about a man name of Charles Cade. He was to stand trial in your court on some charge, I don't know what, but never got here. I was escorting him to turn over to Sheriff Todd, but Cade was killed on our way here."

"Cade," Lawson repeated. "Yes, of course I remember the name. The charge . . . Let me check." He swiveled his chair around, pulled open a filing cabinet drawer, and riffled through the contents. "Here it is," he said after a moment.

The judge turned his chair back to the desk and laid a folder on top of the other papers there. He took a moment to glance inside the folder, then said, "Your man Cade was charged with assault. Something to do with a brawl at one of our local saloons. I remember Jim . . . Sheriff Todd, that is . . . telling me he wanted to use that charge to leverage Cade's testimony about something else."

"D'you know what other case that would've been?" Longarm asked.

Lawson shook his head. "I do not. Jim and I were friends,

and naturally we talked about events in the county, but there were limits. Neither of us wanted anything we spoke about as friends to prejudice my judgment when matters came before my bench."

"Of course," Longarm said. "But Cade knew something . . . about somebody . . . or some thing, and your sheriff wanted his testimony about it. Trading Cade's knowledge for his freedom, I suppose. That's common enough. I wonder if there'd be anything in Todd's records that would tell me more about whatever that was."

"I wouldn't know about that," Lawson said.

"Can I see those office records, Judge?"

Lawson leaned back in his chair again. He steepled his fingertips under his chin and after a moment said, "Let me think about that, Deputy."

"Certainly, sir."

"Come back after lunch, after I've had time to check the county ordinances."

"Yes, sir." Longarm rose and extended his hand to shake again. "After lunch then."

Chapter 23

Martha's Café was just across the street. Georgia Cooper's boardinghouse was a fifteen-minute walk to the south end of town.

Longarm smiled. And began walking.

He was half a block away when he heard screams coming through the open windows of the lady's house. He broke into a run, Colt in hand.

Longarm practically tore the front gate off its hinges and took the steps onto the porch at a single bound. He ran inside to find two men mauling Georgia, one holding her down while the other slapped and punched her. That one had his hand beneath the hem of her dress and appeared to be trying to drag her pantaloons down.

Naughty, naughty by Longarm's lights.

He reached the one on top of Georgia without breaking stride and turned his run into a kick that carried all of his weight on the toe of his black cavalry boot.

The kick crashed into the bastard's nuts. He screamed and passed out from the sudden, unexpected pain, collapsing full length onto Georgia.

The second man was scuttling sideways toward the protection of Georgia's sofa. He threw himself over the back of the furniture and dropped behind it.

Longarm ignored him for the moment and dropped down to kneel at Georgia's side. "Are you all right?"

That was a silly question, he supposed. Hell no, she was not "all right." Her complexion was mottled red where she had been hit. Those areas would likely turn purple and plum with bruising in another day or two. Her hair was in wild disarray and her bodice was torn where one—or both—of her assailants had been pawing at her tits.

"Yes, now that you are here. I . . ."

She did not have time to finish the sentence. Her eyes went wide in renewed alarm.

Longarm swiveled in the direction she was looking. The second man had reappeared above the back of her sofa, and this time he had a gun in his hand.

Longarm was still holding the .45 Colt he'd had in hand when he burst into the parlor.

He pointed it without conscious thought, finger squeezing even as the sights came in line.

He squeezed and . . . nothing.

He looked at his own revolver, aghast, and remembered too late that his own tried-and-true double-action .45 was in the possession of the man who murdered Charlie Cade. Or of the treacherous bitch who took it from him that night on the stagecoach.

In the meantime the would-be rapist was not politely waiting for Longarm to figure out just what gun he had in his hand. Georgia's assailant fired, the gunshot loud in the close confines of her parlor.

Longarm heard the bullet from the man's gun sizzle past his right ear so close he could feel, or imagine that he could feel, the wind from its passage.

That was more time than the man had any right to. Once Longarm had been reminded that he was holding a single-action revolver, he quickly thumbed the hammer back and again squeezed the trigger.

The man's head snapped suddenly backward and there was a spray of blood and brain as Longarm's bullet entered through his eye socket and exploded out the back of his head. The dead man dropped out of sight behind the sofa.

The other one was aware of his surroundings now, although Longarm suspected he was not enjoying them much with his balls pulped. He was still writhing in pain.

Longarm plucked the fellow's pistol from his holster and stuck it behind his own belt, then quickly frisked the man to make sure there were no other weapons he should be worried about.

He rolled the man onto his stomach and handcuffed his hands behind his back, then shifted his attention to Georgia. He helped her to her feet and wrapped his arms around her, giving her what comfort he could. After a minute or so she pulled away from him. She started toward the sofa, apparently remembered what was back there and changed direction to a wingback chair.

Longarm followed and settled on the footstool in front of her.

"Did they hurt you?"

"It hurts where they hit me, but I'll get over it," she said.

"Did they, uh . . ."

"Rape me?" She managed a smile. "I would have thought you could speak plainly. After all, we are not exactly strangers. Not after last night."

"You're right, of course." He took her hands into his and squeezed. "So . . . did they?"

"No. You came in before they could get that far."

"Is that what they came for? To rape you?" he asked.

Georgia shook her head, wisps of flyaway hair dancing in all directions when she did so. "They wanted me to sign something. Wanted me to write out a paper admitting that I don't own any property in the valley. Not this house or my grove or, well, anything."

Longarm frowned. "The property again. That's interesting. I looked at the books in the courthouse this morning. There's no question that the name on the deed is G. Cooper. You said your husband's name is John, didn't you?"

"Yes. John Jason Cooper."

"It seems someone tried to bluff you out of your holdings, and now they're trying to out-and-out steal them. You said something about a grove as well as this house?"

She nodded. "I have a nice little peach grove started. I brought in started trees from Arizona Territory, three hundred of them. They aren't bearing yet, but in another two or three years they should provide me with a nice living."

"Is land hard to buy around here?" he asked.

"Lord, no. Once you get away from town a few miles, it is terribly cheap."

"So if someone wanted to plant his own grove, he could buy land and young trees to start off?"

"Yes. Of course he would have to stay close to the river—that is what gives us the subsurface irrigation—or come up with some other sort of irrigation, flooding or ditches or the like, but even that would be cheap enough. We get all manner of Mexicans up from Taos and Santa Fe every spring looking for work."

"That's interesting," Longarm said. "Will you be all right while I take this asshole over to the jail?"

"I'm fine now."

"Really?" he asked.

She smiled and leaned forward to kiss him lightly on the lips. "Really," she assured him.

"I'll send someone out here for . . . the other one," Longarm said and stood. He took hold of the chain that linked the handcuffs he had put onto the rapist and dragged the man to his feet. The fellow cried out in pain, but there was nothing he could do about his situation except hope that Longarm was not like a normal town deputy, who would more than likely manage to beat the shit out of him on the way to the jail.

"Come along, asshole. An' if you wanta run, go right ahead."

"N-nossir, not me."

Longarm grunted—it sounded as much like a growl as a grunt—and pointed his prisoner toward the door.

Chapter 24

"Where are we going?" the prisoner grumbled. "The jail cage is over there, built in the back of the sheriff's office. I can't climb no stairs, mister. My legs, they're weak. I'm still hurting from where you kicked my cods. I think I'm gonna puke."

Longarm gave the asshole's chain a yank that put him on his knees. He hit the edge of one of the stairs hard. It must have hurt because he howled and began to cry.

"Where . . . ? You can't put me on trial. Not yet. There's stuff I got to do here."

Longarm ignored the man's whining and first knocked on Judge Lawson's door, then pulled it open and shoved his prisoner through ahead of him.

He pushed the prisoner into a corner and kicked the back of his knee to buckle that leg, then did it again to the other leg. He gave a hard push downward on the fellow's shoulder and shoved him to his knees, facing the wall.

"Set there. Stay!"

Lawson looked at his guests with what appeared to be amusement. "What do you have there, Longarm? Surely you aren't taking him for a pet, and slavery isn't legal these days."

"I have a problem, Your Honor. I don't have either local authority or the keys to the sheriff's office and the jail. Which is where I want to put this jasper. You said you'd think about how to handle this now that your sheriff is dead. What've you decided?"

Lawson opened a desk drawer and brought out a steel ring with a half dozen or so keys suspended from it. He stood and leaned forward to hand the keys to Longarm. "Raise your right hand," the judge said.

Longarm did so and the judge added, "By the authority vested in me, Deputy, I hereby appoint you acting sheriff of Tillet County, Colorado. Uh, sheriff without pay, I suppose I should add. The county supervisors would have to approve any remuneration, and they won't meet for another two weeks."

"Do I have to say anything?" Longarm asked. "Like a pledge or somethin'?"

"No," Lawson said with a grin. "It's already done and official." The grin turned into a laugh. "I think. The appointment might not hold up on appeal, but I doubt any defense attorney would think to take it that far. The point is, you now have all the authority you need to look into this matter of Charles Cade." He eyed the prisoner who was cowering in the corner of his office. "And to press the charges against him. Go ahead and put him behind bars and tell the court clerk to record whatever the charges are. But do *not* tell me about them. I have to remain impartial, you know."

"Yes, sir. Thank you, Your Honor."

"My pleasure," he laughed again, "Sheriff."

Chapter 25

"Take your boots off," Longarm instructed. He was holding the prisoner in front of an open jail cell door.

"What? Hey, that ain't right. These floors is cold. I got no socks on. I need my boots."

"Take them off, I said. People been known to hide shit in their boots. Well that ain't gonna work. Not in my jail."

"You're a real son of a bitch as a sheriff, ain't you?" the prisoner complained.

"Coming from a low-life asshole that would rape an innocent woman, I take that as a compliment. Now, kick them boots off, else I'll beat you down to the floor an' take them off for you."

The prisoner grumbled some more. But he kicked his boots off and slid them aside.

"Thank you. Now if you'd be so good as to step inside," Longarm said.

The man did so without balking but said, "You got to take these bracelets off. Damn things hurt, you know."

"In a minute." Longarm frisked him one more time, just to make sure he had no contraband on him, then Longarm

backed out of the cell and closed the iron bars of the door
with a clang. He found the appropriate key on the ring Judge
Lawson had given him and secured the door before he said,
"You can turn around now an' back up close to the bars so's
I can take those handcuffs off."

"It's about damn time."

"Keep talkin', mister, an' I can leave the things on. Let
you sleep in them an' see how they feel come morning."

"Hey, I was just sayin'. Here. Take them off'n me." He
turned and backed up close to the bars.

Longarm fished his own key out of his pocket and used
it to unfasten first one cuff and then the other. He tucked the
key back into the watch pocket sewn into his trousers and
put the handcuffs in his back pocket. "Feel better now?"

"Asshole," the prisoner grumbled.

"I got some questions for you," Longarm said. "Your
cooperation will go a long way toward determining how long
a sentence you get an' where you serve it. Keep in mind
that in addition to bein' the sheriff of this county, I'm also
still a deputy United States marshal. If I like, I can charge
you with assaulting a federal officer. That'll get you fifteen
years in Leavenworth." The truth was that Longarm had no
idea in hell how much time such a charge would bring, but
fifteen sounded like a good enough number.

"Fifteen ye—!"

"Hush," Longarm told him. "Don't go to bitching or the
charges are gonna start to pile up."

"But dammit, I didn't do nothing to you, man. You came
up behind an' kicked me in the balls before I even knew
you was there."

Longarm smiled and said, "That ain't the way I remember it. Way I recall, you tried to kick me first." His smile got
even wider. "Now, who d'you think the judge will believe,

a lying piece o' shit like you or the brave, upstandin' sheriff of this here county?"

"That ain't fair," the prisoner wailed.

"True, true," Longarm agreed with a nod and a grin. "Not fair at all. But that's life, ain't it."

He rummaged through Sheriff Todd's desk until he found paper and ink, then came back and took a chair in front of the iron bars of the cell. "Now, let's see here," he said. "We'll start off with your name . . ."

Fifteen minutes later Longarm yawned and stood. "Thank you for your cooperation, Jerry. I'll make sure the judge knows about it."

He pushed the chair he had been using out of the way and returned to the front of the sheriff's office to take stock of what he had there.

There was the usual pile of Wanted posters from here, there, and everywhere. Many of them he had seen on Henry's desk back in Denver before he ever started out on this supposedly routine assignment.

He found Todd's badge in the top desk drawer and pinned it onto his own coat where it could be seen by all and sundry.

There were two shotguns and a battered old Henry rifle standing in a rack on one wall and a hickory nightstick hanging from that same rack by a thong.

He found an unlabeled quart bottle in a lower drawer. The bottle was about three-fourths full of . . . something. Longarm pulled the cork and sniffed. Then smiled. The liquor was not rye and probably not bourbon. It was a whiskey, perhaps a blend. It smelled good. Tasted mighty good too, he discovered. He was beginning to think he would have liked Jim Todd.

Longarm took another drink, this one in Todd's honor.

And a third to Todd's memory. Then reluctantly he shoved the cork back into the bottle and deposited it in the bottom drawer where he had found it.

A bottle like that, he knew, was an indicator of a man who worked long and worked late. Yeah, he would have liked Todd.

With a sigh, Longarm stood and went out into the main corridor to find the clerk of court and get the paperwork started on the charges against Jerry Hill.

And—he remembered on the way—to arrange for something to be done about the dead piece of shit still lying in Georgia Cooper's front room.

Chapter 26

"What do you want us to do with him?" the young man asked. He and two of his pals were engaged in carrying the corpse—Jerry Hill had said the man's name was Timothy Rand, a slacker who'd drifted in from Taos and had not yet gotten around to moving on—out of Georgia's parlor.

"You got a undertaker in this town?" Longarm asked.

The boy nodded. "Yes, sir, Mr. Thorne. He rents the establishment from J.L. Moore, who owns the cemetery and sells plots there. Moore owns the box factory too, so he makes coffins when they're needed."

"All right. Take Rand to the undertaker. Tell him the county will be paying. Same with you boys. Come by the sheriff's office tomorrow. I'll have to collect your pay from the clerk of court an' pass it along to you."

"A dollar, you said?"

"That's right. A dollar for each of you. Nothing extra for the use of your horse an' wagon though. That's the deal. Fair enough?"

"Yes, sir," the youngster said. "It's fair."

"All right then. You go along. Tell Mr. Moore I'll stop by

some time and sign whatever papers are required."

The boys, and the body, left. Longarm turned to Georgia, who was standing behind him with a bucket of soapy water and a mop. He took her into his arms. "Are you all right?" He felt her nod, her head pressed against his chest.

"I'm fine," she assured him. "Except for the mess. I never knew bullets could be so horribly messy."

"Killing ain't pretty," Longarm told her, "but it's sometimes necessary."

"I suppose so." She was trembling.

"Are you sure you're okay?" he asked.

"I . . . No. Not really. Would it be all right if you just . . . hold me . . . for a while?"

He kissed her forehead, and when she lifted her face to his, he did a much more thorough job of kissing her.

"Would you like to sit down for a bit?" he asked. "You don't have to scrub that stuff right away. It can wait a little while. This evening maybe we can hire a girl to help you with it. Do you know someone who could do that?"

"Yes, I suppose so. I know a very nice Mexican girl who does laundry and cleaning. But I don't have money for things like that, Custis."

"That's all right. I do. Now, come along. We'll sit so's I can hold you. At least until you get over the shakes."

"Where can . . ." She surveyed the gore that was splattered over her wall behind the sofa. "Not here, if you don't mind."

"The bedroom," he suggested.

She gave him a questioning look.

"Aw, that ain't what I'm thinking. If I want t' fuck you, lady, I'll come right out an' ask. I said I want to hold you. That's what I intend."

Georgia managed a smile. Lordy, she did have a most beautiful smile. "If you want to fuck me, Custis, that would be perfectly all right with me. In fact, I would quite like it. But don't tell anyone I said so. It is terribly unladylike, you know."

Longarm laughed. And led her into her bedroom.

They stretched out beneath the canopy on her double bed, and Longarm took Georgia Cooper into his arms again.

After a few minutes her trembling ceased and she began to breathe slower and deeper. He kissed her again then and was pleased to feel her respond with her tongue probing into his mouth and sliding between his teeth and his lip.

The lady was most definitely feeling better.

Her hand strayed to his crotch and began unbuttoning his trousers.

"Wait a minute," he whispered. He stood and stripped off his coat and gunbelt. Vest, shirt, and trousers followed. By then Georgia was out of her apron and housedress. Another moment and both of them were naked.

She held her arms out to him and he knelt between her legs, his dick pulsing with desire.

She was wet. Ready. He required no urging. Longarm lowered himself to her. Georgia reached between their bodies to take hold of his cock and guide him into herself.

Longarm felt the heat of her body as he slid inside the wonderful receptacle she offered.

He bent his head down and kissed her, his mouth on hers as his cock moved slowly in and out. In deeper and out again. In until she sucked up a hard breath that was part pain and part joy. And out again.

"Am I hurting you?"

She shook her head vigorously from side to side. "No. It's wonderful. Really. But until you arrived, I hadn't been with a man for quite a while." She looked up at him and smiled. Ah, that smile. "And never with anyone as large as you are."

He kissed her. And moved within her body yet again. Harder then. Faster. Driving as deep as he could. Until Georgia cried out and clamped her legs tightly around his and with her arms grasped as powerfully as she could around his shoulders.

Longarm let himself go then, humping hard and fast. Feeling the building sap that started in his balls and continued until he could contain it no longer.

The flood of his jism shot up through his cock and exploded inside her pussy, one jet of hot fluid after another until he was sated.

He collapsed on top of her body, Georgia taking his weight easily, as women do with their men.

"Nice," he whispered.

"Lovely," she agreed. "No. Don't pull it out yet. I want to just feel it inside me for a little longer."

"As you wish, ma'am," Longarm said with mock formality. Georgia laughed.

"I wish I had known you when I was younger," she mused aloud.

"Why, Mrs. Cooper, I can't think of a single thing I'd want t' change about you. You're fine just exactly the way you are."

She nuzzled the side of his neck and kissed him there. "Thank you, Marshal Long."

He laughed and said, "It's Sheriff Long if you please. But you can jus' call me 'sir.' "

Georgia sighed and said, "This is so nice I hate to get up."

"But . . . ?"

"But of course we have to," she said. "So if you would be so kind as to get your dick out of me, sir . . ."

Longarm laughed again. "You are an unalloyed pleasure, Mrs. Cooper." He lifted himself off of her.

"Wait here a moment," she said. "I'll get a basin of warm

water so we can both clean up a little before we get dressed. As much fun as it is to enjoy a good fuck, the result is sticky."

"But messy in a nice way," Longarm said.

"Oh, in a *very* nice way, dear man."

Georgia left the room and came back a few moments later with a basin and washcloth as well as a small towel. She knelt beside the bed and washed him before she took care of the juices that were running down her leg.

While she did that, Custis Long left the bed and got dressed, becoming Sheriff Long again when he buckled on his gunbelt and donned the coat with the shiny badge pinned to its lapel.

Chapter 27

Longarm was on his way to the clerk of court's office when he saw Judge Lawson coming down the stairs. He had his coat and hat on and was carrying a brass-headed cane.

"Hold up a minute there, Your Honor. I need to have a word with you."

Lawson stopped, still on the stairs. "You just caught me. I was on my way home for the day. What can I do for you?"

"I need you to swear out a warrant for me, Judge."

"Oh? Something to do with the assault on Mrs. Cooper? I thought you already had that man in custody. The living one, that is. I understand the other one is dead."

"What I'm wanting, Your Honor, is a warrant for the man that hired them other two."

"You got him to tell you? I'm surprised."

Longarm grinned. "All I did, y'see, was to explain to him the difference between cooperatin' and not. Which I figure to be the difference between three years an' fifteen."

"Persuasive," Lawson said.

"Yes, sir. Sure would be to me anyhow. To him too, I guess."

"All right. Let's step inside the clerk's office and I will authorize the warrant. Who did he tell you hired him?"

"Tony Wilson," Longarm said. "According to Jerry Hill, Wilson paid him and Tim Rand fifty dollars each to run Mrs. Cooper out of town. Promised them another fifty once she was gone, and said he didn't care what they had to do to her to get rid of her. Mentioned that he would consider killing her getting rid of her, but he wanted her gone, one way or another."

"Are we talking about Anthony G. Wilson?" Lawson asked.

Longarm nodded. "We are, Your Honor."

Lawson grunted and shook his head. "Good luck getting someone to help you serve the paper. Wilson is quick as a snake with those pistols of his."

"I already seen what the man can do in that regard an' I ain't worried. He's got everybody around here buffaloed, but the feller ain't as bad a boy as he likes to make out," Longarm said. "I don't expect to need no deputies for the likes o' him."

"Well," Lawson said, "even though you are serving without pay, I think I can get the county supervisors to pay for your burial if it comes to that."

"Now, you know," Longarm said, "that is a real comforting thought."

"Glad you appreciate it." Lawson smiled and took Longarm by the elbow. "Come along to the clerk's office then. I'll swear out your warrant and George can write it up for you."

Chapter 28

Longarm tucked his copy of the warrant, properly signed and sealed and ready for service, into the inside pocket of his tweed coat. He walked with the judge out of the courthouse, past the benches, and across the street.

"Good luck to you," Lawson told him. "I certainly don't envy you the job of trying to bring in Anthony Wilson."

"Don't worry, Your Honor. Tony ain't half as bad as he'd like folks t' believe. I'll have him in front of you for arraignment first thing in the morning."

"I just hope you are alive to do it," Lawson said.

Longarm grinned. "I can't argue with that sentiment." The two men shook hands and Lawson went on his way. Longarm paused to slip the Colt Peacemaker from his holster and check the loads. He knew the revolver was fully loaded. It did not hurt to check anyway. He knew a man once who faced down two others in a gunfight, which he won, then went into the nearest saloon to celebrate the event without bothering to reload. That could be done later, right? At the moment a drink with friends seemed more important. Inside the saloon a pal of the dead pair braced him and the gent drew on that one too. Fast. Much faster than the other man. The sound of that hammer falling on empty brass must have been mighty embarrassing to the gentleman in the second or two before he died.

Longarm poked his head into Martha's Café and looked around but did not see Wilson.

"You're not staying for dinner?" John Martha called when Longarm failed to take a seat.

Custis smiled and shook his head. His plans for supper involved Georgia Cooper's good cooking. And quite possibly her other abilities as well. "Not tonight, John. I got a prettier dining companion than you in mind."

"In that case I don't blame you," Martha replied.

Longarm went next to Gaylord's saloon where town marshal Will Gaddis was again leaning on the bar. Or still. As far as Longarm could tell, the man might not have moved from that spot in weeks except to take the occasional piss.

Gaddis looked at the star pinned to Longarm's coat like the thing offended him. "I heard you're our new sher'f," he growled. "That job shoulda been mine, y'know."

"No, I didn't know that, Gaddis, but I'm glad to know that the job *isn't* yours. The last thing this county needs is a useless drunk for a sheriff. It's bad enough the town has one for its marshal."

"Are you calling me a drunk?" Gaddis demanded.

"As a matter o' fact, I am," Longarm said.

Gaddis huffed and puffed and turned red in the face, but that was as far as he took it. He did not have the balls to stand up to Longarm.

"The reason I came in here, Gaddis, wasn't to insult you. I'm tryin' to do my job. Which right now involves finding Anthony G. Wilson. Any idea where he might be at this hour?"

Gaddis ignored him, turning his back and picking up his mug of beer.

Longarm headed for the door to continue his search, but a gent at the other end of the bar stopped him. "I saw Mr. Wilson going into the Chinaman's fifteen, twenty minutes ago."

"The Chinaman's," Longarm repeated. "Where is that?"

"It's the other side of the creek," the fellow said. "Last place on the north end. A Chinaman runs it. Rumor says Mr. Wilson owns it."

"What is it?" Longarm asked.

"A whorehouse. Pretty good one. The Chinaman has some high-class whores. Not the very best we got in town here but pretty good." He chuckled. "They take their dresses off before they lay down for you, and the sheets are changed every day or two."

"Yeah, that's class, all right," Longarm agreed. "Thanks."

Chapter 29

Longarm found a plank bridge across the creek that irrigated the fruit trees in the valley. He crossed over to the other side and walked upstream past a number of small but stoutly built shacks. The last house beside the creek was a one-story, sprawling affair that looked like it had started out as a simple enough shack itself but grew as one addition after another was grafted onto it.

There were several doors on the front of the structure, but a footpath from the public road led only to one. Longarm approached that one and politely knocked.

"A moment, good sir," a voice called from the other side of the door and indeed it was only a moment before the door was opened to him.

A short, very slender man wearing a red silk robe and black skullcap opened the door for him and bowed. The fellow had a pigtail that extended nearly to his waist and a mustache that drooped on either side of his mouth all the way down to his chest. The Chinaman, Longarm thought, in the flesh.

"Ah, new sheriff," the Chinaman said, bowing again, even

lower this time. "Come in, please. We will talk about . . . services. What you offer, what you require."

Longarm was taken considerably aback but recovered quickly enough. He stepped inside and deliberately continued to wear his hat.

Four—no, five; one of them got there late—ladies of the night lined up on display along the wall. They wore only flimsy, nearly see-through jackets and lacy garter belts without stockings attached. They ranged from scrawny to plump and exhibited several hues, none of which looked to be Chinese. There were no beauties among them, but Longarm had seen worse. Hell, he had slept with worse. And likely would again.

"You see," the Chinaman said, "you take. No charge for good sheriff." The guy bowed again. But then making nice with the clientele was what paid his freight.

"First let's talk," Longarm suggested. "How much were you paying Sheriff Todd?" He knew practically nothing about the man, but what little he had heard suggested that Todd was a good man. If he hadn't been, there likely would have been no reason for someone to assassinate him.

The Chinaman made a sour face, his nose curling over his mustache until his mouth almost disappeared in a furry nest of black hair. "Sheriff Jim, bah. He is a stubborn man. You will not be stubborn, no? Twenty dollar a month."

"You insult me," Longarm said.

"My apology, please. Fifty dollar."

Longarm said nothing, and after a few moments the Chinaman said, "Sixty dollar. It the best I can do. First day of month. Every month. Good pay, yes? We deal?"

"And I look the other way when you do what, exactly?" Longarm asked.

"Oh, nothing. I do nothing," the Chinaman said. "You want pick a girl? Any girl, yes? No charge, no charge."

"Another time," Longarm said. "No time this time."

"No girl?"

"No," Longarm agreed. "No girl."

The Chinaman bowed and smiled. "Next time. I go get money now. Sixty dollar. Very good price."

Longarm wondered just what the hell he was being paid for. And whether it would be worthwhile to arrest the China-man for attempted bribery.

He touched the man on the elbow before the little bas-tard could get away, and said, "Later. Right now what I'm needin' is to have a word with Mr. Wilson."

"Mr. Anthony Wilson? Oh, he not here."

"Bullshit," Longarm said. "He is here and I wanta talk to him. Now, tell me where he is or I'll start throwing people out of here until I find him."

The Chinaman looked distressed, but he offered no more lies on the subject. "Please to wait here. I will get." He bowed again and scurried away, his silk slippers making swishing sounds as he glided over the floor.

Chapter 30

Wilson was more than a little disheveled when he finally appeared in the entry hall. He was in shirtsleeves, the butts of his two shoulder holster revolvers glaringly obvious under his arms.

"What do you want, you son of a bitch?" he snarled.

"Now, Tony, is that any way t' greet someone who's trying to do you a favor?" Longarm asked, chiding him.

Wilson's eyebrows went up. "A favor? What favor would you want to do for me?"

"First off, it ain't something that I necessarily *want* to do, Tony. I still don't like you worth a shit. This is more like something that I find that I, well, that I *ought* to do. If you take my meaning."

Wilson practically wet himself with pleasure at that. "The boss got to you, did he? Ha! So now the high and mighty federal man shows his true colors. What did he get you with? It wasn't threats, I bet. Money? Would that be it? Did you roll over for the yankee dollar?"

"You don't need to know everything, Tony," Longarm said.

"Hell, I'm not even going to get mad at you for calling me that. And anyway I'll find out what he got on you. All I got to do is to ask the boss. He'll tell me. I know him. Better than you ever will, I bet."

Longarm shrugged. "I can't argue 'bout that, Tony. But I need you to come with me. You and me got to sit down and chew over a few little things. You know what I mean?"

Wilson nodded slowly. For a moment Longarm thought the idiot was going to wink. As a matter of fact his left eyelid did droop just a little. This was one strange damned crowd, Longarm thought.

Longarm looked around as if inspecting the place, then said, "Not here. I don't trust your Chinaman to keep his ears closed. Come with me over to the courthouse. Everybody's gone home by now. We can have my office to ourselves. Well, alone except for your boy Hill. He's in the cage, but it won't matter if he hears."

Wilson grunted. "I heard you took him in."

"Had to be done," Longarm said. He meant it, but not in the way Anthony G. Wilson probably assumed. "Grab your coat and hat and we'll walk over there."

"All right. Give me a minute." He raised his voice and said something in Chinese.

The Chinaman reappeared so quickly it was obvious he had been lurking—and listening—just out of sight. He bowed very low toward Wilson and bowed again, but not quite so low, to Longarm.

Wilson said something more and waved his hand in Longarm's direction, causing the Chinaman to bow once more. When Wilson left them there in the foyer, the Chinaman said, "Sixty dollar. You want?"

"No time," Longarm told him. "Next time." What the hell. Turn the screws a little. "Seventy-five dollar."

The Chinaman cackled happily, and Longarm realized

the little son of a bitch would have gone higher. A hundred a month at least.

But then Longarm had no expertise when it came to what a proper bribe should be.

Wilson reappeared, this time properly attired except for his necktie, which was missing and probably stuffed into a pocket.

Longarm looked at the Chinaman and said, "Next time. And that skinny redhead too." He was thinking about that fat barmaid back in Denver. That woman was enough to give fat a bad name. "And seventy-five dollars. Next time."

Wilson said something, again in Chinese, and the Chinaman bowed. "Yes, boss sir. One hundred dollar." He bowed again to Longarm and said, "One hundred. Nex' time, honored sir."

"Let's go, Tony," Longarm said, ignoring the Chinaman, as he thought that would likely be proper now that he had been elevated to the status of "honored sir." "We'll stop by Gaylord's an' get us a bottle to take with us if that's all right with you."

"Good," Wilson said. "I keep a private stock there. Very good stuff. I think you'll like it."

"Y'know, Tony, I'm sure you are right about that. Yes, sir, I surely do trust your judgment 'bout that. Go ahead now. I'll follow you." Longarm shepherded Wilson through the door and out into the soft and pleasant evening air.

Chapter 31

"Let me have . . . Say, is that a bottle of Michter's rye I see over there?" Longarm asked.

"Yeah, what about it?"

"Let me have it."

"The whole bottle?"

"That's right." To Wilson, Longarm said, "It's a good rye. Distilled in Pennsylvania but good in spite o' that handicap. Rye is all right with you?"

"Sure. Any good whiskey will do for me."

Longarm doubted that Tony Wilson knew what a good whiskey was or he would not have put it that way, but what the hell. He was not buying the bottle for Wilson anyway.

But Wilson quickly stepped forward and paid for it. He turned his head, smiled, and said, "Since you and I seem to be riding for the same brand now."

"Right you are," Longarm lied. "We'll go far together." All the way over to the jail cell, he thought. But Wilson did not know that yet.

With their bottle of rye safely tucked under Anthony

Wilson's arm, Longarm led the way over to the courthouse and inside to the sheriff's office.

"Mr. Wilson," Jerry Hill called from his cage in back. He sounded excited. "Are you gonna get me out of here? I hope that's what you came for, Mr. Wilson."

Wilson looked at Longarm expectantly. Longarm took the bottle of Michter's out from under Wilson's arm and set it safely aside, then palmed his .45, cocked it, and nudged the underside of Wilson's jaw with the muzzle.

"What the . . . ?"

"You are under arrest, Tony."

"But what the fuck is this about?"

"Attempted murder, that's what. If you hire someone to kill somebody, the law says you are equally guilty of the very same crime. You hired Jerry and his pal to get rid of Georgia Cooper. That means you are guilty of attempted murder." He smiled. "It's really simple. You'll see that when you think about it. Which you should have plenty of time to do."

Longarm lifted one revolver and then the other from Wilson's shoulder holsters and laid them aside, then he patted Wilson down for other weapons. He confiscated a small folding knife, turned Wilson around, and marched him over to the cell, where Jerry Hill was standing close to the barred door.

"Move back, Jerry. I wouldn't want t' get confused an' shoot you by mistake or something."

Hill practically jumped to the back of the cell.

"Good. Now, stay there." Longarm opened the cell door and pushed Wilson inside, then slammed the heavy door closed behind him. He turned the key in the lock and dropped it back into his pocket.

"I'm going to have your ass for this," Wilson snarled. "I am going to see you suffer."

"I'm already suffering," Longarm told him. "It pains me to be in the company of the likes o' you and your toady there."

"There is only one bunk in here," Wilson complained.

"That's true, but there's a good bit of floor. You boys can share that. Now, hold still."

"Where are you going?" Wilson demanded when Longarm turned away.

He stopped and turned back to face them again. "First off, I'm gonna go across the street to Martha's and get something for you boys' supper. Then I'm gonna go back to my boardinghouse and get me something to eat. How's that sound to you?"

"Fuck you," Wilson screamed.

"Asshole," Hill added.

"Say whatever you like," Longarm told them, "but if you make too much noise, I'm gonna have to gag the both o' you an' put you in chains to make sure the one o' you doesn't pull the gag off'n the other. That's, uh, just something for you to think about, both o' you." He turned and headed out into the empty corridors of the Tillet County courthouse.

Chapter 32

Longarm delivered the prisoners' supper—sandwiches; he was not going to trust them with metal utensils—and locked the sheriff's office door before going "home" for the evening. The odd thing was that it really did feel like home to him, at least as much as his boardinghouse room back in Denver.

He hung his hat on the rack beside the front door and went back to the kitchen. Georgia was busy stirring a pot on the stove. She turned and gave him one of those marvelous smiles and held her face up to be kissed. It was a chore he did not at all mind.

"I waited with these last-minute things until I saw you coming," she said, "so dinner will be a few minutes yet. Why don't you go out onto the porch and have a smoke while you wait."

"All right." He kissed her again, gave her a playful slap on the butt, and went out to his preferred rocking chair at the side of the porch. The evening air was soft and his cigar enjoyable. Better yet, Georgia came out to join him a few minutes later. She brought two glasses of brandy with her, handing one to Longarm before she settled onto her own rocker.

"How has your day gone?" she asked. She sounded genuinely interested, so he told her. When he was done, she asked, "Are you ready for supper?"

"Whenever you are."

She stood and offered her hand. He escorted the lady inside and sat at the table while she brought the food and served him. Afterward she asked, "Would you rather read now or," she smiled, "go fuck?"

"Let me think that over, will you?"

Georgia laughed and led the way into her bedroom, shedding clothes along the route. By the time they reached the big, canopied bed she was naked.

Longarm had slept with more beautiful women and women with better figures, but Georgia was . . . He had to think about it for a moment before he realized what it was that set her apart. Georgia was *fun*. She delighted in screwing and she did it well. Because of that she made it all the more of a pleasure for him too.

She helped him out of his clothes and tenderly washed his cock, his balls and his ass before she guided him down onto the bed.

"No, facedown," she said. "That's good. Now lift up just a little. That's right, raise up a little. Perfect."

He felt her hands reaching underneath to stroke his cock and gently fondle his balls. A moment later and he understood why she had washed him so carefully. He felt Georgia's tongue on the underside of his balls. Felt something—her nose?—rub his asshole. Felt her tongue, warm and wet and probing, move from his balls to his ass. Felt her lick his asshole, even penetrate it just a little. The sensation was . . . arousing.

"Damn, lady!" he exclaimed.

He heard her laughter. "On your back now. I want to taste more of you." She giggled. "And I want to take the edge off so when you fuck me you last a long, long time before you come."

"And to do that you will, uh, what?" he asked.

"I will drink your juice, that's what," she said. "Now, do what I told you and roll over so I can get at that meaty, wonderful thing of yours, will you."

He rolled over. Longarm closed his eyes and gave himself over to the sensations of Georgia's mouth. Wet. Warm. Enveloping.

She took him deep into her mouth, her tongue swirling around and around his cock. She peeled his foreskin back and licked the head of his cock like it was an ice cream cone, and when she felt his responses she bobbed her head up and down on him faster and faster, sucking hard, making slurping, gobbling noises, drooling saliva down his shaft and onto his balls.

Until he came. Until he exploded into the wet heat of her mouth.

Then she sucked all the harder, drawing every drop of fluid from him and swallowing it.

And when she was done, when he had no more to deliver, Georgia sat up, allowing his prick to fall away from her lips, and said, "Now, dear man, I want to feel that thing inside me. Move over. I want you on top this time. After that," she laughed again, "after that we'll see."

They would indeed see, Longarm thought with contentment. They would see indeed.

Chapter 33

Longarm was awakened sometime in the middle of the night. He was still in Georgia's bed, and both of them were roused by someone pounding on the front door.

"Stay here," Georgia told him. "I'll go see what they want." She got up and pulled a robe on, lighted a lamp and left the room. She was back moments later to say, "They want you, Custis."

"Me?" He was still a little groggy with the deep sleep he had fallen into, sated after his romp with Georgia Cooper. "Whadda they want?"

"It's Sam Burnett. He asked if the new sheriff lives here. He didn't tell me exactly what is wrong, but he is asking for the sheriff."

Longarm grumbled a little, but he rose and quickly dressed, stepping into his boots without bothering with socks and taking time for neither his vest nor a tie.

Sam Burnett proved to be a mild-looking fellow whom Longarm had seen in the hallway, or perhaps it had been one of the offices, in the courthouse.

"Whatever this is," Longarm greeted him, "can't the town marshal handle it?"

"I'm sorry, Sheriff, but I thought you ought to know about this," Burnett said.

" 'Bout what, exactly?"

"The murders, Sheriff."

"Murders?"

"That's right." Burnett nodded. "We heard shots fired inside the courthouse. We asked Will Gaddis to see what it was, but, well, the truth is that Will is too drunk to go. So me and Troy Jamison went. I have to tell you, Sheriff, I was scared. I think Troy was too. But we went. I mean . . . somebody could've been hurt. You know?"

"You did the right thing," Longarm said. "You say there were murders?"

"Yes, sir. We found the door to your office was broken open. Troy was carrying a bull's-eye lantern so he went in first. We found . . . we found two dead men in there. Inside the cell, they were. Still are, of course. They're lying face-down, so we couldn't see who they are, but . . . Sheriff, whoever you got in that cell, they're stone cold dead now. Shot in the back, both of them."

"Shit!" Longarm groaned. He reached out and grasped Burnett's shoulder. "You did good, man. Thanks."

Burnett looked relieved. "Is there anything else me and Troy need to do?"

"No, I'll take it from here, Sam. Thank you."

Burnett touched the brim of his derby and disappeared into the night.

Longarm carried Georgia's lamp back inside, returned to her room, and finished dressing.

"Trouble," he said. "The men I was counting on to be witnesses are dead."

"Do you want me to fix you something to eat before you go see to this?" she asked.

Longarm shook his head. "Thanks, but I'm all right for now." He smiled. "You already gave me everything I could need." He stroked her cheek and gave her a kiss.

"I'll walk with you to the door," she said. "You'll need the light until you get outside."

"You're a peach," he said. He stopped in what was still technically his room and picked up the sawed-off shotgun, just in case. If you have to get into a scrap at night, he always thought, there was nothing like having a shotgun in your hands.

At the front door he kissed Georgia again and told her, "Lock the door. Folks in town obviously know where I'm boarding, an' I don't want to bring trouble under your roof."

"I'll be fine. You go on now and do your job. You don't have to worry about me."

Longarm headed into town at a brisk pace.

Chapter 34

The lock on the sheriff's office door had been jimmied open using a crowbar or something similar, but the cell door had been too tough a nut for the assassin to crack. If, that is, he even wanted to spring the prisoners out of jail.

What he settled for was shooting through the bars of the securely locked cell. Both Jerry Hill and his boss, Anthony G. Wilson, lay facedown on the stone paving slabs of the jail cell floor.

There was, of course, no sign now of the shooter. He could have been virtually anyone in Buffington, and now Longarm would have no opportunity to get Wilson's testimony about who was behind this sudden murder spree.

The deaths of these two, Longarm figured, pretty much had to be linked to the previous murders of petty thief Charles Cade and Tillet County sheriff Jim Todd.

At the moment, though, he was almost too tired to care.

He could think later. At the moment . . .

Longarm lighted the lamps in the office, then unlocked the cell door and propped it open. He took Hill's body by the feet and dragged it to the doorway, noting with approval that the corpse was no longer leaving a trail of spilled blood behind. Once he determined that the mess was not spreading too badly, Longarm tugged Hill the rest of the way out of the building and down the steps to the little park area in front of the courthouse.

He left Hill there and went back inside to do the same with Wilson.

With both bodies out of the way, Longarm carried a lamp with him while he scoured the courthouse for a mop and bucket, which he used to clean the cell floor before the blood caused a permanent stain.

After he put the cleaning materials away, he took another look around the office. He could not be sure, but he thought the contents of the desk drawers had been disturbed. That would have been the assassin searching for the key to the cell, he assumed. Or it could be his imagination, as he had not paid any particular attention to the way the drawers were arranged.

He extinguished all the lamps except one mounted on the wall in the corridor and closed the office door. There was no way it could be locked now or even latched shut, so he propped it closed with a wastebasket and left it until morning.

Gaylord's was closed, but a saloon at the edge of town named Aces High still showed light through the windows. Longarm walked down there and stepped inside. He was almost surprised to find no sign of Will Gaddis at the bar. But there were five others just like him who were bent over the bar as if they would fall down without its support. For that matter, they might have.

"What will you have, Sheriff?" the bartender asked when Longarm came in. As far as Longarm could recall he had never in his life seen this man before, but the fellow knew who he was.

"Information," Longarm told him. "Who's the undertaker in town?"

"That's Sydney Thorne . . . he's our barber too . . . to handle the laying out. Embalming too if you want it. And Lew Moore owns the cemetery. You buy your plot from him."

Longarm grunted. "Thorne," he said, "where would I find him at this time o' night?"

"Home, I think," the bartender said, "but he won't much like being woke up this late."

"Tough shit. I either get him outa bed just like I had to be rousted out or I leave two bodies lying out in front o' the courthouse steps. By morning I figure they'd both be half eaten away by dogs an' rats an' magpies. Better to get them took care of."

"Two men dead, Sheriff? What the hell is that all about?"

Longarm ignored the question, and after a moment the barman sighed and said, "Sydney won't like this."

"So tell me anyway," Longarm said.

"All right then." He leaned forward. "You can't miss Sydney's place. It's right over. . . ."

The directions were clear enough. Longarm thanked the man and touched the brim of his Stetson.

He noticed that none of the late-night drunks had so much as looked in his direction the whole time he was in the Aces High saloon.

Chapter 35

By the time Longarm found Thorne's house and got the bleary-eyed man on his way to the courthouse to collect the bodies of Jerry Hill and Anthony Wilson, there was a peach-colored foretaste of dawn in the eastern sky and a light showing in Martha's Café.

Longarm walked across the street and banged on the café door until John Martha unlocked it.

"I'm not open yet, Sheriff," Martha said. "Come back in an hour."

"John, I tell you true. I am a man in need of coffee. Bad need."

Martha looked at him for a moment, then stepped back from the door. "Come on in then. But I haven't put a fresh pot on yet. Haven't even got my biscuits in the oven."

"Last night's coffee will do. Is it hot?"

"Ought to be warm anyway."

"Good enough." Longarm took a seat at the counter. Martha poured a cup of ink black coffee that was almost hot.

"Good thing you got here when you did," Martha said. "I was just about to pour this out."

"You are an angel of mercy," Longarm told him after the first bitter taste of the leftover coffee.

"Rough night?"

Longarm told him.

"What will you do about it?" the café owner asked.

"Find the son of a bitch that done this and see that he hangs."

Without being asked, Martha cut a large slab of dried apple pie and set that in front of Longarm. He refilled Longarm's cup and promptly dumped the remainder from the pot then started filling it again with cold water and fresh, ready-ground coffee.

He opened the firebox of his stove and stuffed it full of chunks of split aspen.

"I'm surprised you use aspen to fire your stove. Wouldn't something else burn better?" Longarm asked.

"Damn near anything else would burn better than this shit," Martha said, "but this is what we've got around here. We've used up all the pine within easy reach, and we're too far from anyplace else to haul in coal. We tried bringing charcoal up from Taos, but that's too far and too expensive." He shrugged. "So we use what we can get. And that is aspen, which is fine for making fruit boxes but not worth a damn for firing stoves. The crap burns too quick and not near hot enough." He went out the back door and quickly returned with an armload of the split aspen billets.

"Even this stuff is getting expensive," he said as he dumped the firewood into a large box beside the stove.

Martha felt the side of the coffeepot and grunted. "It's getting warm. Won't be long and I can give you some proper coffee. Do you want something to go with that? Soon as my skillet is hot, I can fry you up some meat and potatoes."

Longarm shook his head. "This pie and coffee are fine, thanks. Damn good pie too." He finished it, took a final swallow of the vile leftover coffee. and fished a quarter from his pocket.

Martha waved it away. "No charge, Sheriff."

"If it's all the same with you, John, I'd rather pay. I don't want there to be any question that I take special favors. Not from anybody."

"Jim Todd was like that too," Martha observed. "He was a straight arrow. We miss him around here. There's talk around town . . . mind now, I'm probably out of line saying this, jumping the gun so to speak . . . but there's talk about hiring you on as our sheriff permanent."

"That's flattering, John." Longarm meant that too.

And actually there were temptations in the idea. Georgia at night and a sleepy county—most of the time anyway—in which to oversee the law during the days.

That would make for an easy life.

A dull one too, though.

Could he really settle down like that?

"Thank you, John." He rose from the stool at the counter and left John Martha elbow deep in a bowl of biscuit dough.

The predawn light was stronger when Longarm reached the street. He turned toward Georgia Cooper's boardinghouse.

Chapter 36

Longarm sat hunched over a plate of bacon and biscuits with
bacon gravy and, much more importantly, a proper cup of
freshly brewed coffee. "Mmm," he said, holding his cup out
for a refill, "this sure beats the mud John Martha had left
over from last night."

Georgia smiled. "Is there any other way I can please
you?"

Longarm slapped her on the butt and gave the nearer
tidy cheek a playful squeeze. "Tonight there is, an' you know
that, woman."

She laughed and turned back to her stove, pulling open the
firebox and placing two sticks of aspen in.

"Tell me something," Longarm mused, "how much are
you paying for your firewood?"

When she told him, he was shocked. He paused to cal-
culate what her small delivery would translate to in terms of
cords of wood and was shocked all the further. "Lordy," he
said, "that's terrible."

"And it isn't even good wood," Georgia complained.
"Mostly we get the leftovers from Mr Moore's box plant.

You know. The bark slices and knots and whatnot. It's terrible, but it is all there is around here, and at that Moore is complaining that he is running out of aspen too now. I don't know what we will all do when the aspen is gone from the hills around this valley. We'll probably have to haul something in all the way from Taos. Wood or charcoal or something. If it comes to that and the prices get too high to pay . . . I don't know what will happen. Buffington may well wither."

She wiped her hands on a towel and sat across from Longarm at the table with her own cup of coffee. "The town wouldn't completely die, of course. We have our fruit trees. Those would bring an income." She shrugged. "But if living here costs more than the income would warrant, I suppose some might actually abandon their orchards and walk away."

"That's terrible," Longarm said in commiseration. "And all because the wood is used up?"

"It sounds like a simple thing, doesn't it," Georgia said, "but think about it. Folks have to have some kind of heat for their stoves if they want to cook and heat for their houses in winter. You just can't get along without those."

She stirred condensed milk and brown sugar into her coffee and said, "It is a problem we are all very much aware of. All of us, everywhere in the valley. Well, everyone except for the bummers, that is. We have our share of those of course."

"Of course," Longarm agreed.

"What will you do about the murders last night?" Georgia asked.

"Why, I'll find the son . . . uh, I'll find the person that done it an' do for him."

"Put him in prison?" she asked.

Longarm nodded. "Or under the sod, whichever way it works out."

"Custis."

"Yes?"

"Would you please fuck me?"

He smiled and stood, abandoning his breakfast and reaching out his hand to her.

Chapter 37

"No, sir, I was sleeping. You can't expect a man to be awake at that hour."

"Not me. Now, leave me alone, willya. I ain't done nothing."

"Oh, I heard the shots, but you should understand that I was inside and, uh, let's just say I was in no position to go outside and look. If you know what I mean."

"No, Sheriff, I didn't see nor hear a thing. Slept right through the whole kit 'n' kaboodle."

"No."

"No, not a thing."

Longarm grunted. He was getting the same story everywhere he looked and from everyone he asked. No one had seen anything and damn few even admitted to hearing the gunshots inside the courthouse.

The story was the same when he saw Judge Lawson on the street and asked him too.

"I'm sorry, Longarm, but I was at home sound asleep. The murderers chose their time well, didn't they?"

"Yes, sir, I'm afraid they did." He walked with Lawson

to the courthouse and followed the man inside, leaving the judge at the staircase to his courtroom and tiny upstairs office, while Longarm continued on to the ground floor sheriff's office.

He pushed the wastebasket aside with the toe of his boot and opened the shattered door.

He had not seen the place in daylight. On the off chance that there might have been something that he missed, he gave the office a good looking over, in particular the area just outside the cell bars. That was where the shooter must have stood. He found nothing of interest. Nothing at all.

Longarm stood where the shooter must have been and peered through the bars to the places where the bodies were when he found them.

Wilson just . . . there. And Hill . . . there.

It occurred to him that only Wilson was shot in the back of the head. Hill's body lay at an angle to Wilson's, and he had been shot in the back but not in the head. The shooter hit Wilson first, probably by surprise, then Hill tried to cower in the corner, but of course there was nowhere for him to hide. That suggested there was only one shooter, not the two or more that Judge Lawson assumed. And that Wilson, probably both of the men, trusted their executioner, otherwise Wilson would not have stood calmly still for his own murder.

The shooter was their boss? Beyond possible, Longarm thought. Likely.

If he was correct that there was only one shooter, Longarm knew, that was definitely not good. It was an axiom of law enforcement that one man might be able to keep a secret, but two men cannot. He hoped like hell that in this case there had been at least two men in the office to do the shooting. More would be even better. They could prop themselves up on some saloon bar and rehash the whole experience. And where there is beer, there are ears to hear all manner of bragging and bluster.

But this time, dammit, he really suspected there was only one shooter involved.

That would make his job harder. So would the fact that Longarm himself was a newcomer here, holding a temporary appointment as sheriff. Everyone in the community seemed to know who he was, but no one here really knew him. They would feel no inclination to open their secrets to a stranger.

But Lordy, he did hate for a killer to get clean away.

It happened, but he did not have to like it.

The good news, he thought, breaking away from the unpleasantness of the early morning, the good news was that he had scrubbed the floor in time to avoid leaving a stain. The spots where there had been blood were dry now and showed no signs of the assassin's work.

Longarm sat down at "his" desk and gave this situation some thought. Someone had wanted Charlie Cade dead. Someone wanted Jim Todd dead. Then someone found it necessary for Tony Wilson and Jerry Hill to die too.

That was an awful lot of murders for one normally sleepy little community.

Farmers—especially fruit farmers—were by nature slow and deliberate, not at all rash or impulsive. They were people who looked ahead instead of back. They planted and were willing to wait for the return on their investment.

And Buffington was a community of farmers.

It made Longarm wonder what was so damned urgent that four lives had been sacrificed to that demand.

Something was going on in Tillet County. Something that Longarm had no idea about.

He sat there brooding about it through what remained of the day. Then he went home to Georgia.

Chapter 38

"That was a fine dinner," Longarm said. "You're a good cook." He grinned and added, "Among other things."

Georgia smiled. "I think I'm supposed to blush now. Or did you have something else in mind?"

"I was thinkin' what you think I was thinkin'," Longarm said with a laugh.

Georgia rocked forward and poured another dollop of brandy into his glass. They were seated on the front porch, relaxing in their rocking chairs as the light faded and evening brought out the whirring of cicadas and chirruping frogs.

It was pleasant. More than pleasant. And if Longarm did not watch himself, this could become a regular thing, almost a ritual. The sort of thing that can soften a man and tie him down.

He held the rim of the glass under his chin and breathed in the sharp, fruity scent of the brandy.

"Georgia," he said, "did you know a man named Charles Cade?"

"I don't think so. Who is he?"

"Was," Longarm corrected. "He's dead now. Taken from

my custody an' murdered. That death is on my head."

"That is why you're here?" She reached out and touched his hand.

He nodded. Took a sip of the brandy. It was not his good rye whiskey, but it wasn't bad. The shit was growing on him, it seemed. Lordy, he hoped that did not mean that he was becoming domesticated.

"Do you want to tell me about it?"

Longarm's brow furrowed, and he took a long, slow breath, then a swallow of brandy.

He told her, finding that in the telling he sorted through it in his own mind as well.

"Charlie Cade was a nobody. Penny ante. You know what I mean?"

Georgia nodded.

"He knew something, though. Something that somebody wanted kept quiet. Sheriff Todd was bringing him back here and wanted to get Charlie to testify to that something. Figured to hold the charges against him as a club to get Charlie to open up about whatever it was. That's something as usually works. A man don't want to spend time behind bars if he don't have to, you see."

"Of course not," Georgia said. "I wouldn't want to go to prison either."

"Todd must've had an idea of what Charlie knew. Otherwise there wouldn't have been need for him to be killed too once Charlie was dead. The pair that held up the stage and took Charlie from me could've ended it right there except for Jim Todd knowing and . . . son of a *bitch*!"

"What is it, dear?"

"I just remembered somethin'. That woman. On the stage. I sat next to her two nights an' a day. Got a plenty good look at her in all that time. Since I got here an' things started happening, Todd being dead an' all that, I've nigh forgot about her. The woman accomplice is the one I oughta be looking for now."

"How would you go about that, Custis? We women find it awfully easy to stay out of sight. We don't spend our time in saloons or sitting around a mercantile smoking pipes and spitting tobacco juice the way you men do."

"Is that the way you women think about us men?"

"Well it's true, isn't it?"

He laughed. "Surely you can't expect me t' agree with such a woman's view of us?"

Georgia smiled, but it was not one of her broad, beautiful smiles. Rather, this one was small and tight and smug. "You don't have to, dear. We ladies know the truth."

Longarm chuckled and finished his brandy. Georgia quickly bent forward to pour a refill. "Seriously, dear," she asked, "how will you go about looking for this mysterious, murderous lady?"

"Everything considered," he said, "I suppose my best bet will be to look in the whorehouses. If she is in one, I'm pretty sure she'd be the boss lady there. From what I recall, she wasn't puttin' on airs. She was the real deal. Had class, if you know what I mean."

"But surely a woman with class would not be in one of those, um, those places," Georgia said.

"You'd be surprised," Longarm told her. "Fact is, I've known a lot o' madams. A number o' them came from what you'd call good backgrounds. And now that I think on it, it makes sense. This woman presented herself well yet she was involved in cold-blooded murder. With that combination of class and viciousness . . . yeah, she might could be in one o' the whorehouses. Would you mind tellin' me where I can find the ones that are here in Buffington?"

"Custis! What in the world makes you think I would be able to tell you a thing like that?"

"Oh, don't give me that shit, Georgia honey. I know you good women always know where t' find the bad women." He laughed. "It's a matter o' self-defense, I suppose, women knowin' where their husbands go an' what they're up to when they go there."

This time Georgia did blush. "I suppose John did go to those places. Still does, I would assume. I can tell you what I know about them."

"And I can tell you," Longarm said, "that your husband is one damn fool son of a bitch to be goin' off to visit some trollop when he has a fine an' lustful woman like you at home. Which I happen to know. And intend to take advantage of again just as soon as I finish this here brandy."

Georgia reached forward, took his glass from his fingers, and held it out to the side. With a smile, one of her good ones this time, she turned the glass upside down, spilling the brandy onto the boards of her porch. "You're finished," she said.

Chapter 39

Longarm waited until early afternoon before he started his round of visitations. Any later and the ladies who ran the cathouses in and around Buffington—and it seemed it nearly always was a woman who was in charge of a whorehouse, the Chinaman notwithstanding— would resent him coming at a time when he might interfere with business. Earlier and they would still be asleep. Longarm did not think he had ever known a whore or a madam who crawled out of bed— woke up, that is; they might get out of bed twenty times a night—earlier than noon, and two o'clock was more common. He knocked on the first of five doors at three.

His knock was answered by a surly, unshaven man who held a spatula in one hand and a diminutive Sharps Ace pistol partially hidden in the other. Longarm had seen the fellow before, drinking in one of the saloons. He had never spoken to him, however.

"You're that sheriff," the man said.

Longarm chuckled and said, "The tone o' your voice makes that sound like an accusation, but as it happens, it's true. I am indeed the sheriff, and I'm here on official business."

"What the hell kinda official business do you got here?" the doorman growled.

"The kind of official business that I'll discuss with the madam of this house." Longarm added, "Unless, that is, you're her."

The fellow's expression tightened, and the knuckles of the hand that was holding the little Sharps went white, but he made no move against the lawman at the door. Which was a very fortunate thing for him, and he probably knew it.

"Come inside an' wait," he said. "I'll tell Miss Evangeline you're here. Can I take your hat? Bring you a drink? Anything?"

"Just Miss Evangeline," Longarm said.

"The parlor is there," the man said. "You can wait in there while I go tell Miss Evangeline you're here."

Longarm nodded. He removed his hat and ambled into the parlor, which was tastefully furnished in blue and silver. There was a fireplace, a well-stocked bar ready for the customers to arrive, and half a dozen furniture groupings where a gentleman could sit with his favorite lady. Longarm chose a seat near the fireplace, which was cold at this time of day, but not for long. He'd barely had time to get settled when a young girl in a maid's smock came scurrying in to kneel on the hearth and build a fire. She seemed to know what she was doing, as she had it crackling within a minute or so.

"Nice," Longarm said when the kid stood up.

"Thank you, sir." The girl curtsied, turned and hurried back out of the room, disappearing into the back of the house somewhere.

Longarm had a gut feeling that he was being watched, but he could not figure out who was watching him or where they were. He waited patiently, not fidgeting or twiddling his thumbs, and after ten minutes or so he'd apparently passed muster, and Miss Evangeline finally put in an appearance.

When she did show up, she breezed into the room and plunked herself down on the settee opposite his. She waved a hand in the air, the hand encrusted with rings and clutching a silk handkerchief, and almost instantly the little serving girl scampered into the room bearing a tray.

"Tea, Sheriff?"

"Please."

They went through the civilized rituals of lacing the bitter beverage with cream and honey and balancing the delicate cups and saucers on their knees, then, the formalities disposed of, Longarm got down to the subject of his visit. Or at least the one he was using as an excuse.

His real mission, to see if the madam of this house might be his mystery woman from the journey down from Denver, had already been completed. And Miss Evangeline was not the woman Longarm wanted to see. Miss Evangeline was in her forties or perhaps a well preserved fifty-something. She was paunchy and bloated enough to be not at all like the woman on the stagecoach.

"I'm told this is the nicest house in Tillet County," he said. "Looking around, I can believe it."

"Thank you, Sheriff."

"I'm mostly here to introduce myself," he said. "I wanted to let you know that I expect you to keep things clean and orderly. No shenanigans if you know what I mean."

"I run a straight house here, Sheriff Long. No man ever leaves anything here that he didn't want to. Nobody gets robbed. Nobody gets rowdy. If they do, they won't be welcomed back and they all know it. I make sure of that. My girls are clean. I take them to the doctor for a checkup every other week. That is a rule in this house. If a girl comes down with something, she has to leave, and if a man has something, he is not allowed to use any of my girls. Every man has to allow the girl to give him a short-arm inspection before they get down to business. There are no exceptions."

Longarm nodded.

"This is the best house in the valley," Miss Evangeline said. "I want to keep it that way."

"Do that an' you and me will have no quarrels." Longarm took a sip of his tea and faked a smile. Lordy, he did hate tea. Horse piss would be just as agreeable to him as the finest cup of tea. Assuming there was such a thing as a fine cup of tea.

He made small talk with Miss Evangeline for a few more minutes, then excused himself and left, passing the male— the bouncer or husband or whatever the hell the man was— on his way out. This time the man had no Sharps pistol in his hand. He frowned and reluctantly nodded to Longarm as he let him out into the mid-afternoon sunshine.

One down, two if you counted the Chinaman's place that Longarm had already seen, and only four more to go.

He had started at the top, Miss Evangeline's whorehouse being recommended to him as the best the community had to offer. It would be downhill from here.

Chapter 40

"Lordy, you should have seen that last place," Longarm said, shaking his head. "Sonuvabitch was filthy. Gave the impression that every whore in the place was likely infected with something that'd make your dick fall off an' the stub rot away t' boot. It made me feel dirty just from standing inside their door."

He and Georgia were once again seated on her porch with brandy and glasses. Longarm's belly was full and his glass was too. He rocked a little, sipped a little, enjoyed the company of this seemingly plain woman who was quite the wild creature once her clothes came off.

"But you didn't find the woman you're looking for?" she asked.

Longarm shook his head. "Sorry t' say, no. I didn't."

"Where will you look now?"

"Damned if I know. I'll think on it. Somethin' will come to me." He grinned. "I hope."

"May I make a suggestion?"

"Of course," he said. He took a swallow of brandy—the

stuff had some kick to it but was altogether too sweet for his taste—and rocked a little more.

Georgia fidgeted for a moment, toying with the strings of her apron, then said, "Practically all the decent women in Buffington and from every farm, ranch, and orchard within twenty miles come to church on Sunday mornings. It would be only proper for me to invite our new sheriff to come worship with us." She smiled. "And if he happened to get a look at each of them while he was doing it, well, wouldn't that be interesting."

"Well I'll be damned," Longarm exclaimed.

"Quite possibly," Georgia said, "but avoiding that is the reason you are supposed to go to church." Her smile turned into a grin. "Finding your mystery woman would be icing on the cake." She stood up. "Which reminds me, I have a nice pound cake you might like for dessert. It's really quite good with some home-canned peaches poured over it. Can I interest you in something like that?"

He first looked around to make sure there was no one nearby who might overhear—there was not—then said, "The kind o' dessert I'm wanting from you, ma'am, has nothing t' do with eating. Licking an' sucking an' fucking maybe, but not actually eating."

"Are you threatening me, sir?" she said, tossing her nose high and feigning a haughty air.

Longarm grinned. "Damn right I am, woman."

"Prove it," she challenged. Georgia turned, her skirts swirling, and went inside.

Longarm came to his feet in a hurry and was on her tail—and soon enough inside it—lickety-split.

Chapter 41

"What's this?" he asked come Sunday morning. Georgia handed him a package wrapped in brown butcher paper and tied with string.

"Open it and see, silly."

He tugged at the string, which only seemed to make the knot tighter. After a moment Georgia laughed and took the package back from him. She bit the string and tugged, and the wrapping came free.

"Well I'll be damned," he exclaimed with a smile. "Is that for . . . You didn't have t' go and do a thing like this."

"Do you like it?"

"Damn straight I do," he said, taking the brand-new white shirt and a trio of starched collars from the package.

"Try it on. You can wear it to services this morning."

"You're fixing to turn me into a regular popinjay, ain't you." But he immediately removed his coat, bow tie, and vest, unbuckled his gunbelt and laid it aside, then unfastened the top buttons on his checked flannel shirt and pulled that over his head, dropping everything onto Georgia's canopy bed.

She handed him the new shirt and he pulled it over his head, undid his trousers so he could tuck the rather long shirttail in, and buttoned up again before buckling his belt.

Georgia stepped close and buttoned the shirt to his throat and helped him fasten a fresh collar in place.

Longarm leaned down to give the lady a kiss, then managed on his own to retie his bow tie and put his vest on.

He reached for his gunbelt, but Georgia stayed his hand with a touch of her own. She shook her head. "It's Sunday morning, dear. We are going to church. Please don't bring a gun into the services."

Longarm hesitated for a moment, then nodded. "All right." He picked up his tweed coat and pulled it on.

Georgia smiled—Lordy, he did like her smile—and said, "You look very nice, dear. Very much the gentleman."

"Maybe so," he said, "but you an' me know that's far from bein' the truth, don't we?"

"Perhaps you are a little too lustful to be considered a gentleman." She giggled. "But we can investigate the possibilities when we get home this afternoon."

"Is there a restaurant open here on Sundays?" he asked.

"Just Martha's Café. John is open seven days a week."

"Then what say I squire m'lady to Sunday dinner after services," he said.

The broadening of her smile was answer enough.

Longarm leaned down to check his image in Georgia's bedroom mirror, then put his hat on and offered the lady his arm. "Shall we go, ma'am?"

Chapter 42

The Community Church of Buffington was on the other side of the creek and roughly opposite the Chinaman's whorehouse, a twenty-minute walk or so from Georgia Cooper's house. As they neared the path leading up to the church doors, Georgia sucked in a sharp breath and her hand tightened on Longarm's arm.

"Something wrong?" he asked.

She pointed with her chin. "The man over there. Coming out of . . . that place."

"I see him."

"That is my husband. That is John Cooper. Oh, please, please don't let him see me with you."

"Relax. I'm your boarder. You're takin' me to introduce me to folks. There's nothing wrong with that, and nobody, him included, needs to think anything more of it than what I just said." They walked on a few steps more, and Longarm thought to add, "If he gets the idea we're sleepin' together, will he cause trouble for you?"

She frowned in thought for a moment and said, "I don't really know. Nothing like this has happened before."

"Well I want you to know that you don't have to take any crap off him. He's the one that walked out." Longarm paused. "Uh, he *is* the one, ain't he?"

"Yes. Absolutely. I was true to my vows every day and every night until then."

"Ever think about divorce?" Longarm asked.

"Every day." She smiled and tipped her head back to peer up at him. "All the more so of late."

They were getting close to the church building, and others, couples and families with children and even a number of singles, were collecting on a network of paths that all led to the front door of the little sanctuary. In addition to the church building with its spindly steeple there was a brush arbor on one side and a set of privies on the other. It was not an especially pretty church, but it seemed to be well attended which spoke volumes about the preacher.

When Longarm saw who the preacher was, he had to laugh. Georgia tried to make the introductions, but Longarm told her, "Me and Pastor Thorne are already well acquainted. He shaved me t'other day and I seen him again when he came to collect those two murdered men outa the sheriff's office cells." Longarm smiled. "It's good to see you under more pleasant circumstances, Pastor."

"Just call me Sydney," Thorne said. "But you remind me. Is there any special service you want said for Mr. Wilson and Mr. Hill? It is too late to ask that about Mr. Rand though. I buried him yesterday afternoon with just a standard Protestant reading."

"I'm sure the same will be fine for them other two, Pastor."

"Sydney. Really. I prefer it."

"I'll try an' remember that, Sydney, an' I'm Custis." The two men shook hands, and Pastor Thorne turned his attention to the next arriving churchgoers. Georgia laid her hand on Longarm's elbow and walked with him into the sanctuary.

"I always sit in the second pew on the far left," Georgia said in a soft voice.

"Go ahead up there if you prefer then," he told her, "but I wanta set all the way in the back so's I can see whoever comes in. That's what I'm here for, remember. D'you want to go up front by yourself or stay back here with me?"

"I'll stay with you, Custis."

Longarm nodded and guided her into the pew, taking the aisle seat for himself while Georgia bent down and retrieved a hymnal from the floor beneath the pew.

There were roughly a score of worshippers already seated, most of them sitting with their heads down, perhaps praying or looking up hymn numbers based on the list posted on a chalkboard at the front of the sanctuary. It was a posture that made it difficult for Longarm to see if any of them might be the woman who'd sat beside him on that stagecoach trek down from Denver.

"Do you see the person you are looking for?" Georgia whispered.

Longarm absentmindedly shook his head, his attention locked on the people already there and the ones who were still coming in.

The flow of newcomers slowed to a trickle and then stopped altogether.

"Well?" Georgia asked.

"No. Not here," he said. "Dammit."

"Custis!" Georgia sounded quite genuinely shocked, even though Longarm had good reason to know that she had something of a mouth on herself. But then that was under other circumstances.

"Sorry." Not that he really was, but it was what he was expected to say. "Reckon this wasn't . . . Whoa! Wait just a minute here."

Up at the front of the room the seven—no, eight—choir members were entering, each of them wearing a matching dark blue robe. The first one in, a woman, peeled off from the main herd and went to the piano that was set to the left of the pulpit. She took a seat on the piano bench, which put her facing away from Longarm.

"I think . . ." He leaned down and whispered into Georgia's ear, "The lady at the piano. Who is she?"

Georgia smiled. "Oh, that's Aggie Moore. Aggie is the wife of what you might call Buffington's leading citizen. Her husband owns the cemetery, the box mill, I don't know what-all else. Aggie is in charge of most of our civic events. Not that there are so awfully many, but she involves herself in everything there is. Why do you ask?"

"Because I ain't for sure, the angle is all wrong and she's a little far away, but I'm thinking she might be the lady that took my shooter and helped with the murder of Charles Cade."

"Oh, no, Custis. Not Aggie. I'm sure of that."

"If you say so, but I'd still like t' get a closer look at her."

"That won't be a problem, dear. After the service we can walk around back. I'll introduce you to all the choir members and you can speak with Aggie."

Longarm grunted.

"You will see, Custis. It can't possibly be Agnes Moore, Mrs. Jesse Moore."

He smiled and squeezed her hand. He did not, however, blindly accept Georgia's assurances on the subject of Mrs. Moore. "Later," he said.

Chapter 43

"May the Lord's face shine upon you until we are together again, beloved." Pastor Thorne lowered his upraised arms and the congregation all came immediately to their feet. The church was filled with the scrape and shuffle of shoes and the buzz of conversation as the people began to flow toward the front doors. Several people moved instead toward the front, where Thorne was standing.

The choir, Longarm noticed, had filed out through a back door, their pianist going with them.

"Do you want me to introduce you to Aggie?" Georgia asked, now in a normal voice instead of a whisper.

"Yeah I do," Longarm said.

Rather than buck the flow of moving people, Longarm and Georgia Cooper joined them, and once outside, they walked around the side of the church, toward the back, where the choir robes were stored in a lean-to addition at the rear of the building.

They found the seven ladies of the choir standing there chattering happily as they hung their robes on a long pole.

Georgia approached the women and asked, "Where's Aggie?"

One of the ladies said, "You know, honey, that's the funniest thing. As soon as we got outside, Aggie took off running just as fast as she could go."

"She didn't even stop long enough to leave her robe," another said.

"She's still wearing it."

"Probably took it home to clean it or . . . or something," one of them suggested.

"Anyway, she isn't here. Maybe at home." That one stepped close and put an arm around Georgia's shoulders. "We heard what happened at your house the other day. Are you all right, dear?"

"Of course I am, thanks to Sheriff Long here. Custis, I would like you to meet . . ."

Longarm was impatient to go see this Agnes Moore and determine once and for all if she had been that woman on the stagecoach down from Denver, but there were social requirements attached to a sheriff's badge that did not exist for deputy United States marshals, so he smiled and nodded and smiled some more, until all the palaver about the gunfight inside Georgia's house was taken care of.

Then he said, "Could you show me where the Moores live, please?"

"Of course, Custis." Georgia excused herself from the others, took his arm, and said, "This way."

The town's cemetery lay behind the church, past a screen of cottonwood trees, and the Moores' house just beyond the cemetery.

"You don't mind walking past gravestones, do you, Custis?" Georgia asked while they were still in the cottonwood grove.

"Not s'long as none of them is mine," he told her. "I

seem to remember being told that Moore owns the mill and box factory. Where are they?"

Georgia pointed. "Right over there. You'll see them once we get into the cemetery. Aggie's house is there." She pointed again. "And the mill is practically next to it but in that direction. He owns quite a bit around here, you see. Peach and pear orchards too.

"They weren't wealthy when they came here, but J.L. worked very hard and, I understand, got very lucky in a card game. He won some land. Made that pay by starting the cemetery and selling burial plots, then started the other businesses and expanded his land ownership with the money he made off those cemetery plots."

"Seems an odd base for a fortune," Longarm said, "but by damn if it works for the man, good for him. That's free enterprise at its best."

"They have so much, but I'm told that Jesse still seems driven to succeed," Georgia said. "Like he doesn't have enough already and has to grasp for more. That's such a shame. He was such a nice young man when he first came here." Georgia sighed.

"It's funny the way success affects some men," Longarm said.

"Funny?"

"Odd," Longarm corrected. "You see that sometimes. A man gets a taste of wealth an' of a sudden there's no such a thing as enough."

They left the line of cottonwoods and came to an ornate metal fence marking the boundaries of the Buffington cemetery. Longarm opened the gate and let Georgia go through ahead of him, then followed and dutifully closed the gate behind him. Any gate, anywhere, how you find it is how you are supposed to leave it.

"I think . . ."

He never had a chance to finish his sentence. His words were cut short by the angry zing of a bullet passing close to his head and a moment later the dull, booming report of the gunshot.

"Down," he yelled, grabbing Georgia and taking her to the ground with him.

Chapter 44

Longarm's hand swept down to his belt and back . . . empty. His revolver was back at the house, lying on Georgia's bed.

"Dammit!" He pushed Georgia's shoulder, urging her flat atop a slightly mounded grave. "Stay down."

"But you . . ."

"I'll be fine. Now, you do like I tell you and stay the hell down. I'll be back in a few minutes."

Longarm lifted his little .41 derringer out of his vest pocket. Aiming it was complicated by the fact that it was soldered onto his watch chain, but the little gun had a big bark and there were times when a loud noise was enough to do a job. Not that this seemed like one of those times, but Longarm just plain felt better having a gun, any sort of gun, in his hand at the moment.

He deliberately kept his hat on, wanting it to show above the granite headstone where he and Georgia were sheltering, then raised his head high enough to see around the side of the stone.

Another shot rang out, the bullet clipping the top of the

headstone and whining off into the distance in the direction of the church behind them.

"Ah, there you are," Longarm mumbled, glaring toward the puff of white gunsmoke that marked the position of the shooter.

He again reached down to give Georgia a reassuring touch on her back, then gathered himself and sprinted for the next tombstone.

The gunman fired a third shot. This time the bullet came close enough for Longarm to hear the sizzle of its passage through the air. He lifted the derringer on its tether and squeezed off one of his two shots toward the puff of gunsmoke forty yards or so ahead. His object was not to kill— although that would certainly be a welcome fluke—but to let the son of a bitch know that Longarm intended to attack, not just hide behind one grave while waiting to be put into one of his own.

Longarm jumped up again. And immediately dropped behind the next tombstone as a fourth slug passed overhead.

Immediately he was up and running. Straight toward his attacker.

The son of a bitch saw him coming and panicked. He left the protection of a parked wagon and ran.

A second figure, unexpected, jumped out and ran with him.

Longarm was fairly sure he had never seen the man before, but he did more or less recognize the person who was with him. That was the church pianist, Agnes Moore. It would have been difficult for him to mistake that fact as she was still wearing her deep blue choir robe.

If Longarm had had his Colt, they both would have been dead by now. They were certainly in range of it. But not of the derringer, which was essentially a belly-to-belly sort of firearm.

Longarm stopped running, took aim as best he could, and loosed off his last cartridge. It did no good, nor had he really expected it to. But it made him feel a little better. Then he stood helpless while Moore and his missus—it pretty much had to be them, he believed—disappeared behind their house, only to reemerge moments later on horseback, taking off at a mad gallop south through the orchards that bordered the town.

With a sigh, Longarm turned back to collect Georgia Cooper.

"Are you all right?"

"Yes, of course," she said. "Are you?"

"Pissed off but not hurt. Come along. I got t' go down to your house for my guns, then I got t' figure out where I can find a horse to use."

"Sam Chance, my neighbor, has some very fine horses. I'm sure Sam would loan you one."

"Good. You can ask him for me while I throw some things into a bedroll. I might be gone for a spell. But first I wanta go over there behind the house so's I can get a look at the tracks left by their horses, see if there's anything distinctive I can look for when I go to tracking them."

Longarm took Georgia by the arm and urged her along at a more rapid pace.

Chapter 45

Longarm touched his heels to the flanks of Sam Chance's sleek gelding . . . and the damn thing blew up beneath him, bucking and leaping and trying to turn itself inside out. Longarm clamped his jaw tight shut so he would not bite his own tongue and clamped his legs even tighter around the barrel of the tall bay horse.

The horse snorted and blew snot and began to sunfish. The shotgun that Longarm had slung from the saddle horn flew off and hit the ground muzzles-first. That impact jarred the hammers and the left barrel discharged, sending the shotgun sailing high into the air and sending the bay into a frenzy of pure terror.

Longarm stayed with the crazed son of a bitch just as long as he could enjoy it, then bailed, pulling his feet from the stirrups and allowing the horse's powerful gyrations to eject him from the saddle. He managed to land on his feet but toppled over backward onto his butt.

Chance caught the bay before it could bolt for freedom. Longarm got up off the ground. He brushed himself off. And tried to ignore Georgia, who was doing her level best to hold in a huge belly laugh. Longarm grinned. "Go ahead. I know it's funny."

She burst out laughing, and so did Sam Chance.

"What do you think, Sheriff? Do you still want him?"

Longarm shook his head. "I appreciate your generosity, Sam, but the animal is a mite too flighty for the work I got in mind. I don't think I'd want t' be on top o' him if I got to do some shooting."

"If that's what you have in mind, Sheriff, my wife's buggy horse is one I got from the army's Remount Service. They took an ice pick to its eardrums and now it's deaf as a post. Steady though. No kind of noise can make it spook. Goes well enough under saddle, although it does have a hard mouth. You're welcome to the use of that one if you'd rather."

"I'd rather," Longarm admitted, his pride being considerably less important than an ability to get the job done.

"Then let's switch your gear off of the bay. It's that plain brown standing over there by the water trough."

It took only a minute or two to shift the saddle from the bay to the brown. Chance did that while Longarm retrieved his shotgun, checked it for any obvious damage, and reloaded the left barrel. Once Chance had the saddle secured on the brown, Longarm draped the thong he had tied onto the shotgun over the saddle horn and checked to make sure the borrowed saddlebags and blanket were secure as well.

"You have spurs?" Chance asked.

Longarm grinned. "Sure. Back home in Denver. Didn't figure to need them when all I set out for was a stagecoach ride down and back."

"You'll need spurs for this old boy," Chance said. "Just a minute." The helpful fellow disappeared into his barn and emerged a moment later carrying a pair of manure-caked spurs with the rowels wired so they did not roll. Schooling spurs, Longarm thought. They would do the job just fine.

He knelt down and strapped them onto his boots.

Longarm thanked Chance again and stepped onto the brown. The horse stood steady, its ears twitching back and forth.

Georgia came over to stand beside his right stirrup. She reached up and touched his hand. He wanted to lean down and give the woman a kiss good-bye, but in public like this he could not do it without destroying her reputation. Instead all he could do was touch the brim of his Stetson in salute and hope she understood. Hell, that situation was something she would surely understand better than he.

"G'bye, Sam, and thank you for the use of your animal. Miz Cooper, don't be letting my room to nobody else 'cause I expect to be back in a few days and reclaim it."

"It will be waiting for you, Custis." She smiled. "That's a promise."

Longarm touched the spurs to the flanks of the brown and pointed the animal south.

Chapter 46

Longarm's lips thinned in a tight smile. He was not at all surprised. The Moores' tracks led due south through the soft earth of the fruit orchards around Buffington. They were easily followed. Quite as if Moore and his wife deliberately chose to ride across soft ground.

Which as a matter of fact they had.

"You're gonna have to do better than that if you want to shake me off'n your trail," he mumbled aloud.

The trail veered away from the creek and entered a thick patch of sage and, a little higher on the slope above the water, some low spreading juniper.

"D'you see it, old boy?" he said a half hour later. "Your nostrils is flaring. You can smell this trail, can't you? You're like a damn bloodhound. Good. You can help me keep on them."

Longarm drew rein and tried to think it through. Had the Moores turned east here? Or west. He was sure they would have gone one way or the other now that they had established—or thought they had—their direction of travel as being to the south. And of course he knew damn good

and well they had not swung back around to the north or he
would have spotted them.

The brown horse, unbidden, turned its nose east, back
toward the mountains where Longarm first encountered the
pair. He was convinced that Moore was the unseen holdup
man who stopped the coach, and Aggie Moore was his traveling companion along with Charlie Cade on the way down
from Denver.

"You smell something, you ugly sonuvabitch? Well I believe it, boy. You might be deaf, but your nose works just
fine. All right. We'll go the way you say." He reined the
brown left and nudged its flanks.

Half an hour later they reached the shallow creek that
watered the valley. Hoofprints showed plain on the muddy
fringes of the streambed. This was where the Moores crossed.

Rather than plunging on after them, Longarm dismounted
and let the brown drink while he knelt and dipped water in
his palm to slake his own thirst.

Once the brown had had its fill of water, he led the horse
aside. He loosened the cinch and lifted the saddle and blanket to allow cooling air to reach the animal's back, then he
reset everything and tugged the cinch snug.

"Good enough," he mumbled as he swung back into the
saddle and nudged the horse into motion, splashing across
the creek and up the slope on the far side.

"Now let's see where we go from here," Longarm said.

He very nearly felt sorry for J. Lewis Moore and Agnes
Moore. They apparently had little experience running from
the law, while he had years of experience at being on the
back end of such a chase.

He figured to catch up with them shortly after dark. By
then they should believe they had gotten away clean.

They would be wrong about that.

Chapter 47

Stupid, stupid, stupid, Longarm thought as he reined the brown a little to the left and spurred the horse into a trot. There was no need now to worry about trying to follow a trail. He could see plainly enough where the Moores were headed.

The pair had circled wide around Buffington after laying what they seemed to consider to be a false trail, then they'd cut into the hills toward the coach road where Longarm first encountered them. Apparently they intended to take the public road on their flight back toward Trinidad or Pueblo.

Perhaps they thought they would be allowed to run free if they got away from him here. Perhaps they thought he would not follow. Perhaps they thought it would be safe to return to their wealth and comfort in Buffington if they only could escape Longarm now. Perhaps they simply did not think. Custis Long did not know, did not have to know. All he was concerned with was catching these two who were responsible for the murders of Charlie Cade and Jim Todd, Jerry Hill and Anthony G. Wilson. Everything else would be up to Judge Albert Lawson and the courts.

Rather than trying to track the Moores through the foothills and into the mountains, Longarm cut across to the road and put the brown into an easy lope. To his mind that beat hell out of pushing his way through aspen thickets and scrub oak jungles.

Six hours later, just as the sun was sinking into the horizon, he reached the nameless mining camp where he had first found succor following the stagecoach robbery and Charlie Cade's murder.

The wide-assed gray dray horse seemed to recognize him when he stripped the saddle off the brown and turned it into the pen behind the blacksmith shop.

"Hello, Pansy. Did you miss me?" He rubbed the big horse's poll and scratched the hollow beneath its jaw.

He poked his head into the smithy and said, "Hello, Gerald. I just turned a brown horse into your corral. Wanted you to know about it. I hope you don't mind. Here, d'you want me to work those bellows for you?"

Gerald grunted and said, "No need. I'm finishing up here. Thanks though."

Longarm waved to the man and went on to greet Bonner McGuire in passing on his way to the chuck tent. The same skinny fellow was cooking and the same kid serving the same son-of-a-bitch stew. Longarm already had his quarter out ready to give to the kid.

"Did you remember to bring a spoon this time?" the boy asked.

"Nope. Have t' borrow yours again," Longarm told him.

The kid shrugged and went to get the cup of stew, a cup of coffee, and a spoon to go with them.

But this time Longarm laid the sawed-off shotgun on the table beside his meal and chose a seat that allowed him to look out onto the road that ran through the camp.

The tent was filling up as evening came on, but no one chose to sit close to this armed man who was sitting among them.

Chapter 48

"Would you like a refill on that coffee, mister?"

"Yes, thanks, I . . ." Longarm grabbed the boy's arm and turned him to face the back of the tent. "Quick now. Get yourself out back an' don't come out front again, for there might be shooting."

The kid's eyes lighted up as if he thought shooting would be a fine treat rather than a threat.

Longarm had no more time to worry about the boy. He had the shotgun in his hands as he ducked out of the tent into the road.

Two horses were approaching. And two riders that he very well remembered. One of them he had sat next to most of the way down from Denver.

Longarm positioned himself in the middle of the road, shotgun across his chest and hammers cocked.

"Hold it," he said as the riders approached, obviously unaware of the danger that lay ahead.

"Oh, my God!" the woman yelped. "It's . . . How did you . . . Oh, Lord."

Longarm nodded. But did not tip his hat to the lady. He

did very politely say, "You play the piano real nice, ma'am. I did enjoy hearing it at services this morning."

The man, who Longarm presumed was her husband, scowled. "You have no right to detain us. Please stand aside."

"Mister, I have every right. You've committed murder against the laws in Tillet County, of which I am the sworn sheriff. Furthermore you committed an assault on a federal officer, resulting in the murder of a prisoner under his . . . that is to say, my . . . care and responsibility. Those charges are more than enough reason for me to take the both of you in for trial. Now, hand over your weapons, please."

"We don't have any weapons," the man declared firmly, "and if we did, that is our right."

"Mister, you were shooting at me back in the Buffington cemetery. I don't figure you'd've got rid o' your guns since then. Now drop 'em."

Moore's horse fidgeted, prancing and turning sideways. Deliberately, Longarm was sure. Moore was getting himself into position to shoot his way out of this confrontation.

"If that gun o' yours comes out of the leather, mister, you will regret it," Longarm warned him. "Now, drop it. Right onto the ground."

"I will. I will," Moore said. "I will."

But he wouldn't. He grabbed for the butt of his revolver. Apparently it was his best effort at a quick draw.

He was not faster than the hammers on Longarm's shotgun could fall.

Longarm tripped the front trigger of his twelve-gauge, and the muzzle blast lit up the twilight for yards around.

Moore was blown completely out of his saddle, the force of the buckshot driving him back onto his horse's rump. There he toppled sideways and fell headfirst to the dirt beneath the horse's feet.

"Don't be going anywhere," Longarm warned Agnes Moore.

"I won't. I . . . Oh." Aggie Moore slumped in her saddle. She took hold of the horn and tried to lower herself to the ground, but her strength failed her and she very slowly buckled until she was lying beside her now dead husband.

Men who had been watching nearby rushed to help the lady dressed in a choir robe, but Longarm warned them away. "Don't trust her," he said. "She'll be armed too. You boys stay back."

Longarm stepped forward, carefully, and bent over Mrs. Moore. Enough daylight remained that he could see for sure now that she was the woman who had ridden with him and Charlie Cade on the coaches down from Denver.

He could not be certain that Moore was the man who'd stopped the coach that day and ordered Cade off, but it was a reasonable assumption.

"Miz Moore. Aggie. Can you hear me?"

She shifted her gaze from her dead husband's face. When she spoke her voice was a faint whisper. "You, you son of a bitch."

"Yeah, everybody tells me that. No, now, don't you be reaching for no gun there. Let me have it."

The weapon he pulled from a pocket in her skirts was his own double-action .45. It needed a cleaning but otherwise seemed to be all right, and he was pleased to be able to return it to his holster where it belonged. The Peacemaker he'd gotten down in Buffington could now be bartered with Bonner McGuire.

"You got any more guns on you?"

She ignored the question, so he assumed she did not. She did not look lively enough to be a threat anyway. Still, she was apt to come out of this faint spitting and wanting his hide, so he needed to make very sure she was not armed with any . . . Oh, yes. He remembered now. The lady had had a derringer that day. It should be somewhere on her person too.

It took a minute, but he found the little pistol hidden in the bodice of her gown. He wondered if she had taken it to church with her or if she took time to grab it and his Colt before they bolted for freedom.

"Miz Moore. Can you hear me? What the hell for did you and him do all this?" He had to shake her shoulder to get her attention, which seemed to be wandering even though she was awake. Groggy but awake. "Miz Moore?"

"You really . . . don't know?" She winced. He could see no reason for her to be in pain, yet she seemed to be.

"All these killings," he said. "No, I really don't know why you done them."

"Coal," she whispered. "Fortune in coal. We would . . . would have been rich." She shuddered and held herself stiff.

"Is coal all that valuable?" he asked.

Agnes Moore did not answer, but apparently she and her husband had thought it was.

Longarm shook her shoulder again, but he might as well have been shaking a shoulder of fresh pork. The woman was as dead as one.

It took several minutes for him to find the reason why. A stray pellet from the spray of buckshot out of his sawed-off, a pellet aimed at her husband and not at her, had hit Aggie Moore beneath her left tit and brought her down, likely from internal bleeding, since there was not much that showed on the outside.

"What's this all about, Marshal?" Bonner McGuire asked, probably on behalf of all the others in the camp. "Why'd you kill these folks?"

"Murder," Longarm told him. He shook his head. "Murder and greed. They was already rich, but they wanted more.

Stupid." He stood and looked around at the men who were gathered close. "Tell you what, fellows. Let's drag these bodies out o' the road an' put the horses in Gerald's corral. Come morning, I'll throw them over their saddles and haul 'em back to Buffington."

He got back to town in mid afternoon and tied his string of horses in front of the courthouse, with the bodies draped over them. A crowd immediately began to collect to gawk at the sight of their leading citizens dead in the street.

"Pastor," he said to Sydney Thorne, who had come out of his barbershop to join his fellow townsfolk at this unusual sight, "would you please get Judge Lawson. You can tell him that I'm resigning as your county sheriff."

"Where are you going?"

Longarm grinned. "I gotta go tell a nice lady that she's all of a sudden rich." On the ride down from the mountains he had concluded that the coal had to be on Georgia's land, otherwise Moore and his crowd would not have been so insistent on gaining possession of the young peach orchard. "I'll be back directly, then we can get these sons o' bitches buried in some o' their own cemetery plots."

He was in a good mood when he stepped back onto Mrs. Chance's buggy horse and headed for Georgia Cooper's house.

Watch for

LONGARM AND THE BLOODY RELIC

the 390th novel in the exciting LONGARM
series from Jove

Coming in May!